PALE SHADOWS

DOMINIQUE FORTIER

translated by
RHONDA MULLINS

Coach House Books, Toronto

First English-language edition. Originally published as *Les ombres blanches* by Les Éditions Alto, 2022.

Coach House Books acknowledges the financial support of the Government of Canada for the translation of this book. We are also grateful for the generous assistance for our publishing program from the Canada Council for the Arts, the Ontario Arts Council, and the Department of Canadian Heritage through the Canada Book Fund.

LIBRARY AND ARCHIVES CANADA CATALOGUING IN PUBLICATION

Title: Pale shadows / Dominique Fortier ; translated by Rhonda Mullins.
Other titles: Ombres blanches. English
Names: Fortier, Dominique, author. | Mullins, Rhonda, translator.
Description: Translation of: Les ombres blanches.
Identifiers: Canadiana (print) 20230556450 | Canadiana (ebook) 20230556469 | ISBN 9781552454688 (softcover) | ISBN 9781770567863 (EPUB) | ISBN 9781770567870 (PDF)
Subjects: LCSH: Dickinson, Emily, 1830-1886—Family—Fiction. | LCGFT: Novels.
Classification: LCC PS8611.O7733 O4313 2024 | DDC C843/.6—dc23

Pale Shadows is available as an ebook: ISBN 978 1 77056 786 3 (EPUB), ISBN 978 1 77056 787 0 (PDF)

To François Ricard, with my infinite gratitude,
this book for whom he was the first reader

The absence of the Witch does not
Invalidate the spell —

EMILY DICKINSON

*B*orn December 10, 1830, in Amherst, Massachusetts, Emily Dickinson died May 15, 1886, in the same home, having spent the final years of her life cloistered in her bedroom, keeping up a voluminous correspondence and writing hundreds of poems she refused to have published in her lifetime.

I wanted to imagine her existence in Paper Houses (Les villes de papier). Then, one year later, I needed to write the story of the women who survived her, and who in a sense brought her back to life: her sister Lavinia; her best friend and sister-in-law Susan, Austin Dickinson's wife; Mabel, Austin's mistress; and Millicent, Mabel's daughter, a child at the time of this story.

Lavinia brushes her sister's hair one hundred strokes, mahogany hair with no trace of grey; she pulls it into a chignon that is not severe or uncomfortable. She is wearing one of her white dresses. Lavinia chooses her prettiest shoes, patent leather, with a low heel. Shoes meant for dancing. Then she searches Emily's features, runs her finger along the ridge of her nose. The skin of her purple-veined eyelids is so thin she can almost make out the dark pupils beneath. Behind the eyelids, her eyes are still alive.

Emily's lips are closed; her teeth can't be seen, any more than her bones, all the secret ivory that skeletons and the living are made of. In death, Emily seems taller than in life, perhaps because lying down takes up more room than standing. She looks no older than thirty-five – death has taken years off her age.

Lavinia replaces a lock of hair, straightens the lace collar one last time, then moves the bible the maid considerately set on the table. Emily won't be needing anything to read.

Instead, Lavinia goes out to the garden and comes back with an armful of flowers. She braids the violets into a necklace that she ties around her sister's neck, then slips two heliotropes still warm from the sun between her icy fingers, accompanied by a note that says: *For our dear friend, the Reverend Charles Wadsworth.*

Even in death, one must be courteous.

࿎

It is not, as custom would have it when someone prominent dies, the notables of the town who will carry the coffin from the hearse to the church, then to the cemetery.

'No notaries, no doctors, no professors,' Emily had commanded, a few days before her death.

Not content just to drive them from her bedside, she wanted to be sure they would not pursue her to the great beyond, refused to see her body turned over to the pale hands of lawyers and doctors, accustomed to contracts and stethoscopes. She wanted to be carried by the same arms that, day in, day out, carry the apples, the milk, and the straw.

Lavinia respected her wishes. It is labourers and farm workers who carry the white coffin. They stand so erect, so little weighed down by their load, it is as if the coffin contains nothing but a few handfuls of hay.

Mabel leans over the coffin. After having long played the piano in the Homestead parlour for Emily, who would be hidden away in her room, and after having collected, like treasures, the small offerings Austin's mysterious sister sometimes sent in thanks, this is the first time she is seeing her with her own eyes. Emily looks twenty years younger than she is. Her skin is like marble: smooth, cold, flawless. Mabel is not surprised. She suspected that Emily had spent years secretly becoming her own statue.

The dead woman in the white wood coffin is wearing a white dress, and for a moment Mabel wonders whether the body hides other layers of white: lungs, guts, a heart of snow.

She feels breath on her neck and knows without turning that Austin is standing behind her. Everyone knows, and all eyes are riveted on them. People can't help but look at lightning, or a drowning. We look at eclipses, even though we know they can strike us blind.

Susan, Austin's wife, bosom friend of the deceased, spent two days and two nights writing the obituary that appeared in the *Springfield Republican*. She hadn't written for months, and it required considerable effort, like an invalid trying to get out of her armchair to set off down a long road. To take up her pen, she had to shed the weight of recent years, find the woman she used to be, lively and confident, the young woman to whom Emily wrote hundreds of letters, all carefully preserved. With greying hair, a thick waist, but a beating heart, it was an old young woman of twenty who sat down to write about her dead friend.

She poured everything she knew about Emily into the text, polishing sentences until they gleamed, choosing each word from among ten, like one would collect only the most beautifully coloured agates from the beach.

As she passed on in life, her sensitive nature shrank from much personal contact with the world, and more and more turned to her own large wealth of individual resources for companionship, sitting thenceforth, as someone said of her, 'In the light of "her own fire."'

That was true, but it wasn't quite right. Susan was never satisfied. No eulogy could ever do Emily justice; it would have to have been composed by the bees or the robins, written with the pale ink of the clouds. Or leave the page in the newspaper blank.

Her task completed, the burial behind her, Susan shuts herself away in her sorrow as if in prison. It is no wonder that in French the same word is used for the penalty imposed on a criminal and the grief caused by the loss of a loved one: *la peine*, the sentence, the pain.

Lavinia returns from the cemetery at the end of the afternoon and closes the door behind her. The emptiness swallows her whole. The house is not big enough to hold such sorrow. She walks through the rooms, from the kitchen to the office, by way of the parlour, the dining room, and all the bedrooms, and in each one she throws open the windows to let in the May evening, along with the robin's song.

The silence is deafening, punctuated by the tick-tock of the clock. Mechanically, Lavinia opens the housing of the tall grandfather clock from which Emily refused to tell time for so long; she plants the key in the face, winds the clock. The pendulum has never stopped swinging left to right, but Lavinia continues to turn, even when the key resists and comes to a stop. She persists until the mechanism gives way and time stops circling the white face.

Without getting undressed, she curls up on Emily's bed. The linen sheets still smell of her sister, a blend of sour milk and vanilla, similar to the fragrance of the heads of newborns. She sleeps straight through till morning.

❧

The next day, she is awakened by the call of a robin perched on the windowsill where dewdrops bead. If she could look at a drop closely enough, in it she would see her face upside down, the whole bedroom on its head.

The robin, one of the familiar birds that Emily had been in the habit of feeding each morning, continues to appear for its daily bread. Lavinia takes from the nightstand the remains of a dry biscuit, which she crumbles between her fingers. She opens the window a crack, places the crumbs on the sill, watches the bird who watches her back before starting to peck. Its orange chest, round and velvety, is her second sunrise.

Everything is identical and nothing is the same. The house is like a theatre set that could blow away at the slightest gust. Each room is strange, as if it had been recreated on a slightly different scale, with cardboard walls, as if its orientation had been imperceptibly altered and the light no longer came through the windows at the same angle. The bedrooms have that impersonal quality of rooms you enter for the first time and that mean nothing. Life has left them, and they too have died. How many people does it take to make a hearth, a home? Do cats count?

In the afternoon, Lavinia takes from the icebox the chicken Mr. and Mrs. Mercer left for her. The bird is plucked, gutted, and dressed. The offal – burgundy heart and liver, kidneys the size of cherries – is wrapped separately in paper; she will make pâté tomorrow. She stuffs the cavity with a chopped onion, a carrot, and a bouquet of thyme and rosemary, rubs the skin with lard, seasons it with plenty of salt and pepper, and grates a quarter nutmeg over the bird. All that is left to do is to tie the wings and the tips of the legs so they don't burn when roasting, then put it in the oven. One hour, two hours, three hours; now and then she takes out the bird, bastes it with its juices, and puts it back in the oven.

Soon a delicious fragrance wafts through the house. Lavinia steams potatoes, puts peas on to boil, the first of the season. She sets the table: one plate, one knife, one fork, one napkin, one glass of water.

She transfers the vegetables to serving bowls, takes the chicken from the oven, places it on a platter, and carries it to the dining room. The skin is roasted and crispy, perfectly golden. Ceremoniously, using a long carving knife, she separates the wings, which she places on her plate with a new potato and a handful of peas. She forces herself to chew, swallow, repeat.

When she is done, left on her plate are half the potato and some peas, a whole wing, which she strips of its meat to give to the cats, who have not missed a single one of her movements.

Then she takes the rest of the chicken, and rather than covering it and placing it in the icebox to keep, puts the whole thing on the back porch, an offering for the creatures of the night – raccoons, possums, hungry ghosts.

What should be done with Emily's clothes? Lavinia doesn't dare give them away; it would be a betrayal. She is frugal and refuses to throw them out or put them in storage. Things are meant to be used. What if she were to make a quilt from her late sister's dresses, skirts, and blouses? Pleased to have found something to keep her busy, she sets out on the bed everything Emily owned upon her death, which is next to nothing. She had always known this next to nothing is all white, but now it sinks in. Who has ever seen an all-white quilt? One might as well sew the snow that blankets the fields with thread made of clouds.

Sighing, Lavinia gently folds the clothes, as one would tuck a child into bed.

Of her sister's effects, Lavinia sets aside a small number of objects she can't imagine either keeping or giving to the poor. A doll Emily loved as a child, her writing case, her kaleidoscope.

Austin stops by at the end of the afternoon as he sometimes does – not so much because he has anything to tell her or the desire to see her, it seems to Lavinia, but because he wants to postpone going home to Susan at Evergreens. Sitting in front of a glass of iced tea, he turns the kaleidoscope with his fingers.

'Do you remember that Christmas?' Lavinia asks.

He shrugs. 'I'm not sure. How old were we?'

'You must have been around thirteen. You got a stationery set, and I got a sewing kit. I resented you so.'

He is stunned. 'Why on earth?'

'Because Father and Mother never thought I could string three words together, much less write a letter of any interest. The sewing box held the promise of mending and darning; I wanted to throw it on the fire.'

'But I thought you liked needlework?' Austin asks, still stunned.

'Well, I did use it to learn to embroider. But I was still dreaming of binoculars, or a globe. Something that lets you see far.'

Austin tries to recall the Christmases that followed, when he continued to receive books as gifts, while his sister was given ribbons and pretty silk thread. 'I have a globe at home. Would you like me to lend it to you?' he finally asks.

Lavinia bursts out laughing.

Somewhat offended, he stands. Pointing to the kaleidoscope, Lavinia suggests, 'Take it to the children. It will amuse them.'

He prefers not to remind her that Edward and Martha are past the age for this sort of toy and leaves wondering what else he might not know about his only surviving sister, who he believed had no secrets.

Austin brings Emily's kaleidoscope to Millicent, Mabel's daughter.

The little girl murmurs her thanks, jams the eyepiece to her eye, and her breath is taken away. She gently turns the golden ring, and the room breaks apart, is divided and reflected, flipped on its head. She suddenly feels like she can see all the stars her astronomer father keeps talking about and that she struggles to tell apart. Once these stars have entered the bedroom, they will never leave.

She keeps the kaleidoscope under her bed, in a box with her most treasured possessions: a perfectly intact cicada moult; a robin's nest; a rough, black stone David brought her from the side of a volcano, as big as her fist, full of holes, and as light as a ball of wool; a playing card (the king of clubs); a pine cone; and a dictionary, which is her kaleidoscope, the prism through which she sees the world.

❧

In his library, her father has the twenty volumes of the fourth edition of *Encyclopaedia Britannica; or, a Dictionary of Arts, Sciences, and Miscellaneous Literature*, books bound in caramel leather with yellowed pages that smell like the leaves carpeting the floor of the forest where Millicent likes to lose herself.

She plunges into it with the same delight other little girls reserve for arranging the furniture in their dollhouses; it is an entire universe, but shrunk to her size, that she can explore at her leisure. The long scientific terms don't put her off. On the contrary, she notes them carefully to look them up later in her dictionary, but soon realizes that she can guess the meaning from their Greek, Latin, or French roots. They are little puzzles to pull apart to assemble their meaning.

Her first word, at barely one year old, was the same as all babies: *mama*. But the second, a few days later: *book*.

The first time Austin truly saw Mabel was in hearing her. He had already spotted her from afar, the wife of the new astronomy professor at Amherst College, but he wouldn't have been able to pick her out from the wives of the other faculty. People said she was pretty; in theory he had no opinion on such matters. He had been told that she played the piano, so he invited her to play at Homestead at the insistence of Lavinia, who had few sources of entertainment.

She had sat down at the instrument in the Dickinson parlour, dressed plainly, back straight, delicate neck with stray locks that formed a lather of hair, her fingers curved prettily over the keys, and had played the first bars of a Chopin nocturne. Lavinia had quickly closed her eyes to listen more deeply. As for Austin, he was caught up in tracking the musician's slightest movements. When she started to sing to accompany her playing, her voice flutelike and true, a shiver ran down his spine.

Meanwhile, Mabel kept time without missing a beat, with a precision that was entirely mathematical. It was not that she was not feeling the music – she enjoyed certain symphonies well enough – it was simply that she was more sensitive to the effect she was having on the audience, on the brother and sister sitting together in the parlour. But that evening she was also playing for a third, invisible spectator: Emily, upstairs, who for a moment had pressed her ear to the wooden floor to better hear the melody that rose up to meet her, before returning to the other music she heard in the silence of her room.

❧

A few years earlier, Mabel had not been thrilled about the idea of moving to Amherst, which, compared with the bustle of Boston, seemed horribly narrow and provincial. But that was where David had been offered a position as a college professor, a stable job, well-paid, albeit without glamour or any real opportunity for advancement. She could not help but be a bit disappointed – she had expected more from a man who had a passion for the stars and the endless mysteries of the cosmos.

They had nonetheless packed up books, furniture, and clothing. In truth, they didn't own much, and to see their existence sealed in a few boxes had revived in Mabel the profound feeling of dissatisfaction, a lack of fulfillment inspired by even her greatest successes, and especially by those of her husband.

David, however, had come home enthusiastic from his first day at the college. He had exuberantly sketched for her, through gesture and imitation, a portrait of all his colleagues, as well as the school's administrators, among whom the figure of Austin Dickinson stood out: the treasurer, a cultivated man, a lawyer from one of the most prominent Amherst families, who seemed to reign over everyone with quiet authority.

Two days later, the wife of one of the professors had come to call on Mabel to give her a tour of the town. The chubby woman with pink cheeks and twinkling blue eyes brought to mind a porcelain doll, but she was a well-informed guide, who had at her fingertips the official and unofficial history of the town. After showing her the location of the general store, the milliner, the tearoom, and the post office, she had taken her down the prettiest streets to admire imposing homes bathed in the patrician shade of maples.

'Who lives here?' Mabel had asked, before a large square house in pale brick, trimmed with forest-green shutters.

'That's Homestead, the Dickinson home,' Samantha had announced with the same tone she might have used to say: it's the White House. 'The first brick house in town. Only two sisters still live there, Lavinia and Emily.'

Then, lowering her voice, 'Emily never leaves the house. They say she even refuses to come out of her room. She dresses all in white, summer and winter, and she writes poems, oh … poems …'

The woman stopped short, as if words were not enough to describe the beauty of Emily's poems, then she went on. 'But she shows them to virtually no one. Can you understand such a thing? Why write, if it is to remain secret?'

She must not be so wonderful if she chooses to stay hidden, Mabel thought to herself, but, her heart beating, she was already wondering how she could become known to and loved by this eccentric creature. She made a gesture with her head that could express either ignorance or agreement, then, pointing to a second home, almost as beautiful as the first, she asked, 'And that one?'

'Ah, that's also a Dickinson home, Evergreens. It belongs to Austin, the college treasurer. He is Lavinia's and Emily's brother; he married Susan Gilbert. They live there with their children Martha and Edward. Their little Gilbert has passed on. The house is the height of luxury – just imagine, they have everything, even an icebox in the kitchen. And Susan hosts the most sumptuous evenings you could hope for. Do you play piano?'

'A little,' Mabel said, in a tone of false modesty.

'Well then, you will have to try theirs. It's the best in town.'

Everywhere she looked, she was in the realm of the Dickinsons.

∾

A few weeks later, when she accompanied David to a soiree at the college for professors and their wives, administrators, and students' families, Mabel immediately recognized in the crowd the tall silhouette of Austin Dickinson, whom she had never seen.

He stepped up on the stage for his welcoming remarks, and voices quieted even before he indicated he wanted to begin. Tall, broad-shouldered, his back slightly hunched, he stood with an unconscious grace. He had black hair, a high forehead, inky eyes, a natural authority that made people whisper in his presence. She had thought he looked like her idea of Lucifer before the fall: the most powerful of angels. In that moment, while he was advancing under the stage lights, all eyes glued to him, it was all over: she had invented him, dreamed him so well that she was already hopelessly in love with him.

The evening went by in introductions and lively discussion; invitations flowed from all quarters. As usual, Mabel was a hit. Not once did Austin look at her, even though she kept a keen sense of where he was in the large, packed room. But she could already tell; this man who didn't yet know her name was the one through whom, finally setting aside poetry, theatre, and journalism, even the piano, she could devote herself to her greatest work, at last becoming what she knew herself to be since childhood.

In the following days and weeks, every time David spoke to her about Austin or she heard his name uttered in town, something deep in her breast reverberated like a small chime, a bell that she carried within her that marked the rhythm of her steps with a secret little song: *Dickinson, Dickinson, Dickinson*.

When their bodies came together for the first time, the thin boundary that separated them dissolved – a layer of skin falling. From that day on, however things appeared, they were like burn victims, flayed alive. After their embrace in a deserted Homestead, under the transparent gaze of Dickinson ghosts, each had gone home to write in their diary the name of the new two-hearted creature they had become, entwining the letters of their first names as earlier they had entwined their limbs: *AMUASBTEILN*.

Austin transferred a plot of land to Mabel and David so they could build their home. It was Austin, working with David, who drew up the plans, suggesting that a back staircase lead directly from the garden to the second floor where the bedrooms were. In seeing their two heads bent over the large sheets that detailed the elevations (facade, back view, sides, porch), she had a feeling she would have been at pains to name, but pride had a definite place in it.

Two centuries earlier, a maharaja madly in love with a favourite who had died tragically young had built a white marble palace in her memory. Mabel had not one but two men for herself, who were working together to build her a house – all while she was still marvellously, prodigiously alive.

Her house was called The Dell. It was brilliant, scarlet red.

The funeral over, nothing left to do, Susan sinks into her exhaustion. She is too tired to even worry about *that woman*. She is heavy with everything she misses, burdened by all she has lost to death or to lies: Emily, Austin, Gilbert.

Her grief inhabits her like love: burning, ravaging.

She rereads Emily's letters as if trying to discover something she had not seen before. No matter what she does, every one of them is a goodbye. Surrounded by the envelopes, Susan feels even more alone than at the cemetery. She would give all these dead letters in the blink of an eye to hear the true voice of her friend again. And yet, as she unfolds the yellowed sheets, she finds Emily's face or, more accurately, something like a reflection or a shadow, the trace she left on her life, a sort of memory crystalized around the void – a fossil.

One day Emily had written that November is the Norway of the year. It was in that grey, icy month, neither fall nor winter, that Gilbert, at just eight years old, died forever.

Since then, Susan has lived only in Norway.

Two or three times a week, she leaves her house and walks with a determined step, without stopping, to the cemetery. She doesn't dare look at Emily's grave, goes to briefly greet her parents, before sitting in the cold grass, back against the gravestone with the engraved name of her little boy, who sleeps beneath the earth. She takes from her bag *The Adventures of Tom Sawyer*, his favourite book, and starts to read aloud. They are on page 107. It's the fifth time they have read it together. Sometimes, when she catches her breath between two sentences, she forgets for a moment that Gilbert can't hear her.

Lavinia stretches out between the sheets after having snuffed out all the lamps, put out the fire, closed the windows, and locked the doors. She is alone with Cinnamon and Pepper, who are too lazy to go outside and are stretched out beside her. She closes her eyes, forces herself to keep them closed; she counts: one, two, eight, twenty sheep, but sleep won't come. She opens her eyes; the bedroom is plunged in darkness, the world has kept its shape but lost its colour. Is this how we see when we are dead? she wonders, just as she hears the floor groan at the other end of the hall, a faint but unmistakable noise, the sound of a floorboard creaking under someone's – or something's – foot.

She pricks up her ears, curious, but not remotely alarmed. Lavinia doesn't really believe in ghosts, and she believes even less in robbers. Like her, the cats listen, their ears mobile, turning toward the source. Another floorboard creaks, and Lavinia recognizes the sound, about one step from the first, slowly advancing toward her: it's Carlo, Emily's dog, who died a few years before his mistress.

࿔

In the desk in Emily's bedroom, the pen is deep in sleep, dreaming of the words it has left to write and invisible poems it traced in the sky when it was a goose on a long journey. It recognizes its luck; it has lived two lives.

The down mattress yearns for the weight of a body. It feels so light that it could fly away, one feather at a time, spreading in the ether like July clouds, dissolving like salt in water.

The ink has hardened in the inkwell. It turned to jelly, paste, then a puck; its cracked surface has greyed, covered with a velvety film like the skin of some mushrooms. It sits there, inanimate, a stone. It has returned to the mineral world.

The desk used to be a huge oak, with branches that touched the sky. It was home to families of birds and a gang of raccoons. On stormy evenings, it creaked in the wind like the mast of a ship. They started by cutting off the top; the highest limbs fell in a rustle of leaves, nests dislodged, fragile shells broken, then average-sized branches, and finally the fourth or fifth largest ones, as thick as a man's torso. When all that was left was the trunk, it was carved up into large sections from which they cut the golden boards that became the desk. When it was done, all that remained was a stump on which the history of the tree, its one hundred and one winters, could be read in concentric circles. The desk misses winter. It would like to know snow one last time.

Emily had told her several times to burn her letters and diaries, and Lavinia never thought she would disobey her. It was just that, so far, she had been unable to carry out her wishes. This morning, she pushes on the bedroom door, enters noiselessly, for a time is immobile in the sun streaming through the window. Pepper chooses the moment to slip between her legs and stretch out in the middle of a square of light outlined on the floor. Nothing has changed, but the silence isn't the same. The room is filled with her absence.

She opens the bottom drawer of the mahogany chest of drawers: rolled stockings, petticoats, sleeveless chemises. All but the stockings are ghostly white. Nightshirts sleep in the second drawer, the third is home to handkerchiefs, collars, and a few scraps of lace. That is where the diaries sit, which she throws into the fireplace without a glance, like dead birds. A flame rises, almost white from the ardent light.

Once the diaries are consigned to the fire, it is the turn of the letters, piled in the second drawer from the top. Lavinia takes out the bundles tied with black, green, forget-me-not ribbons. Dried flowers, leaves, and clovers fall from the envelopes. She doesn't open them. May they keep their secrets in the casket of their yellowed pages. But some come unfolded on their own, like morning glories at dawn, and then she reads, despite herself, the first words:

> *My dear Emily …*
> *Emily dearest …*
> *Dear lady of the House …*
> *My love …*

She folds them back up quickly as if to prevent the words from flying away, scattering; she abruptly tosses them in the hearth. They make the reddest flames.

Then Lavinia opens the last drawer. This triggers an avalanche of scraps of paper, blown by an invisible storm. Pieces of torn envelopes, corners of flour bags, scraps of sugar packaging, paper remnants in which spices are wrapped, bits of lists, fragments of music scores all take flight like a swarm of seagulls. They spread the fragrance of cinnamon, chocolate, soap, and black pepper.

Lavinia grabs a scrap of paper, the first her fingers happen upon, where she can barely make out a few words – she would need her glasses – but she knows by instinct, suddenly, from the goosebumps that prickle the skin of her arms, that it's a poem, just as one knows immediately, in putting one's hand in the fire, that it is burning.

The scrap of envelope trembles between her fingers. Paper has never been so alive.

Her first impulse is to put everything back in the drawer. She feverishly collects the bits of paper, makes piles, and pushes them aside, but it is a lost cause; they seem to have multiplied, or the drawer has shrunk. The poems no longer fit in it, will not fit in it ever again – has anyone ever managed to send the snow back up to the clouds, lava back into the volcano, tears back into eyes?

૪ᐧ

Kneeling at the foot of the bed, she lifts the top of the camphor chest, like those in which girls collect items for their trousseau: chemises, tablecloths, sheets, handkerchiefs. Between the wood planks, Lavinia discovers dozens of handwritten booklets, each a few pages thick, their white pages sewn by hand with the same regular petit point used to suture flesh after a wound.

She opens the first with infinite care – it is like spreading ribs to reveal the red mystery beating below. The pages are filled with Emily's fine handwriting, so pointed it is hard to read, bird tracks on a frosted surface. For a moment, Lavinia fears that the sheets will melt in her fingers. At the same time, she senses that this fragile snow will outlive her – that it will outlive them all.

Without knowing it, the woman alone in a bedroom was making one of the most important decisions in American literature. If, out of fear, fatigue, laziness, calculation, incomprehension, or love for her dead sister and respect for her last wishes, she had decided to do the same to Emily's poems as she had done to her letters (and what is the difference, in the end, between the former and the latter? Are poems not simply letters to an unknown recipient?), no one would remember Emily Dickinson's name today. If not for Lavinia, Emily would have died like a tree falling in the forest when no one is there to hear: no sound, no echo.

But did she have the right to want to make a book of Emily's poems, when Emily had refused to publish them during her lifetime? Her sister was never shy to ask for – to demand – exactly what she wanted. If she wanted Lavinia to throw her poems in the fire too, why didn't she instruct her to do so? Was it because, unable to decide, she had left it up to her younger sister? But Emily never let anyone choose for her.

We can imagine Lavinia searched for days for instructions, dug through every pocket, overturned the mattress, probed the gaps between the floorboards, shook books to dislodge anything hidden between the pages. In vain. Emily had left her body of work and her sister to their own devices. Or she had given them the gift of entrusting one to the other.

Lavinia Dickinson is cut from the same cloth as Max Brod, who chose to ignore the last express wishes of his friend Kafka, who had made him promise to throw his papers into the fire without reading them, as Otto Frank, who resolved to make public the diary of his daughter who died at Bergen-Belsen. Lavinia is one of the rare authors of chance to whom we owe gratitude for the monumental works they did not write.

How many people does it take to make a book? How many beings does each of these people contain, how many ghosts? And what if it were the ghosts who were writing? When I say 'I', who is speaking?

A part of me keeps getting loose, escaping. Rather than try to stick it back to the rest, I fly off in pursuit fifteen, twenty times a day. I make meals, I drive the car, I put away clothes, but this other part of me walks through the house deserted by Emily, looking for a word or an image. It's like trying to remember bits of a dream hours after waking, or trying to snatch bundles of fog with your hands; all of it, this fragile stuff, keeps slipping through our fingers.

In my head, continually, there is this little piece of muted music, most of the time impossible to put down on paper, the melody hard to make out, scrambled by all the interference. How does it feel to be *whole*, every part reassembled? Is it marvellous or frightening to feel oneself fully exist, in one place? Why do some beings need to live several lives at once, in worlds of their own invention? Is it because they do not have the knack for living just one life properly?

Emily assembled forty fascicles, like the number of days Our Lord spent in the desert. As for the poems, Lavinia gives up counting, but they are too great in number and volume to fit in one or more envelopes. For a moment she considers piling them in a large paper bag, but that seems deeply improper, a serious breach of etiquette, although she would have been at pains to say why. A milk crate would not do either, nor the carpet bag in which she stores her embroidery thread, hoops, balls of wool, and knitting needles. The chest is too heavy; it would take two to lift. Porcelain is transported wrapped in old newspapers, oranges in tissue paper, new dresses carefully folded in half in large cardboard boxes, but what on earth do you carry poetry in?

For lack of a better idea, she finally gets a cardboard suitcase from the attic, the one Emily used during her last stay in Boston. She carefully lays the poems in it, as if they could be broken or bruised; she can't help but feel like she is taking her sister on a trip.

What she isn't asking herself, not yet, is what is the appropriate thing to do with Emily's other missives, which number in the thousands, written over the course of her lifetime to those she loved, sometimes without having met them, and which are now scattered to the four winds. Shouldn't they too be committed to the flames? Until they are reunited, or destroyed, isn't her sister scattered in a thousand pieces in as many strange houses?

༂

The next day, Lavinia goes to see Susan, who knew Emily better than anyone, the preferred recipient of hundreds of letters exchanged between neighbours, house to house. Her sister-in-law has heavy lids, lifeless eyes. It is as if she were disguised as her mother, even her grandmother.

'I need help,' Lavinia announces.

Susan barely turns, keeps looking out the window at the view of nothing in particular. No doubt she is awaiting the return of Austin, who is off at that woman's house again.

Lavinia starts over, and in a strong, clear voice, says, 'Well, it's not really me who needs help. I've come to see you about Emily.'

Susan shudders. A shadow passes over her face, hardening it a little more. The Dickinsons keep letting her down in every way possible: they deceive her, they lie to her, they cross over to the other side. This time won't be any different. And yet, she can't say no.

༂

Emily's poems are bolts of lightning, flashpoints on which Susan burns her hands and her eyes. She spends the morning and then the afternoon slowly reading them over, sometimes holding the same lines cupped in her palm for twenty, thirty minutes, squeezing so tight that she feels blood beating in her fingertips.

They form the short verses of a secret gospel. They are magic formulas. Speak them in the right order, with the right rhythm, and a dove appears, a flame from a hat, a wreath of daisies; say them backwards and grasshoppers rain down, the sun splits in two, the stars go out in the sky, the world is extinguished.

❧

At the end of the day, Susan makes an effort, even several: she puts on her periwinkle dress, the one with the puffy sleeves and the fitted waist that shows off her figure; she puts blush on her cheeks. She roasts a pheasant, prepares a purée of Jerusalem artichokes, peeling one by one the tubers that always make her think a little of children's feet. She even bakes an apple pie, its aroma of cinnamon filling the house when Austin finally opens the door, after seven.

He seems irritated to find dinner awaiting him; normally he prefers to take a cold tray up to his office, where he remains until Susan has gone to bed.

'Where were you?'

'I was working.'

It's not true, and she knows it. She can smell that woman's perfume from ten feet away, so why doesn't he at least take the time to make up something plausible she can cling to? Is she not even worth a lie?

'On what?'

He shrugs. 'It wouldn't interest you.'

They sit at either end of the table, two strangers. The pheasant is a bit overcooked; the flesh is dry under the fork. Austin eats without looking up from his plate. With obvious effort, he asks in turn, 'And you?'

'I spent the day with Emily.'

She indicates the pile of poems on the buffet. Austin shudders. He stands, takes a corner of a torn envelope, reads a few lines, looks at Susan as if he has just noticed her presence.

'I didn't know she had written this much,' he says, in a flat voice.

'Lavinia has decided to publish them,' Susan tells him.

He raises his eyebrows and sets down the fork that was still in his hand. 'I'm sorry?'

'Well, since Emily expressly asked her to destroy her letters and didn't mention the poems, it can't be against her wishes.'

Her wishes. At one time, Austin could read his sister's mind, like clear water. And she never thought to inform him of the existence of her poems.

'Why are you the one telling me this? Does Lavinia want my approval?'

'No, not especially.'

'Then what?'

'She asked me to help her prepare them for publishing.'

Susan expects to hear objections, questions, even mockery, but he simply asks, astonished, 'Really? Why you?'

This is said without meanness or acrimony, without an afterthought. He is genuinely perplexed. And his perplexity that someone has chosen her, her, for an important task, the incredulity at the trust that has been placed in her pains her heart in a way she no longer thought possible.

In a note her friend sent her some forty years before, Susan reads: *We are the only poets, and everyone else is prose.*

What has she done with the poem of her life?

Austin takes his lover's fingers in his, a doll's hand in a bear's paw. Both are still trembling, 'two cords that continue to vibrate after the last note has faded,' she says, and he is moved that she is a pianist down to her abandon.

'My love,' he says, 'I wish I were twenty so I could marry you.'

Mabel has a soft, crystalline laugh.

'But I already have a husband,' she points out in that mischievous tone that drives him mad. She pulls back to trace, with her nail, the ring on Austin's finger. The band has been there for so long that the finger has shrunk between the first and second phalanx, like a tree that has been encircled by an iron hoop and has continued to grow above and below the constraint.

She drives her point home. 'And you already have a wife.'

Austin sighs. Is Susan really still his wife? The creature with whom he increasingly rarely shares his dinners has so little in common with the girl he married thirty years before. Is she the same person? Or are people one day replaced by the worst of themselves?

He tries to slide off the gold wedding band that is strangling his ring finger, but the ring won't slip over the joint. Mabel watches him struggle for a moment, and then, slowly, she takes his finger in her mouth, wets it with her saliva, and gradually slips the precious metal along the even more precious skin. She holds out the ring to him, and he tries it on each of her slender fingers. Too big. He ends up slipping it on her right thumb.

'You may not be my wife in the eyes of the law, but you are my wife in the only ways that matter.'

She doesn't answer, unsure she wants to belong to anyone, but dizzyingly pleased by the gift, the symbol of it. She will proudly wear this ring, even if everyone in Amherst will recognize it, having seen it for years on her lover's finger. She will wear it *so that* everyone will recognize it.

It is only in the middle of the night, while she is struggling to fall asleep beside her husband, that Mabel wonders whether the ring on her finger that was exchanged years earlier with another woman does not mean in some cryptic, monstrous way that she has just entered into an alliance with Susan.

Mabel throws nothing out, ever. As if trying to document her own existence, she carefully keeps, sorts, and organizes tickets to concerts she has attended, invitations, notes received, drafts of those sent, preserving even the ribbons around sprays of flowers she is given, toiling like a maniacal archivist on a work that she would like to be infinite, the book of her life.

Above all she keeps letters from her many admirers, which she stores in a pink cardboard box tied with a silk ribbon. She takes them out every few months to review the contents. In almost geological strata, there lie the testimonials of those who over the years paid tribute to her beauty, her spirit, her intelligence. In rereading these testimonials, she finally feels like a character in a novel. Which is to say, she feels like she really exists.

Within this collection she has been accumulating since childhood, a handful of letters are worth more than all the rest. If she had to save only a few, it would be these, short and wild, scribbled by Emily Dickinson, behind her bedroom door, to thank her for having played so beautifully in the parlour. In unfolding them, she feels herself momentarily lifted up to the celestial storey from which Emily is no doubt still listening.

Just one of these notes is perhaps a little less dear to her, the one about Millicent, whom Emily, after having spotted only once, described as that *quaint little girl with deep eyes, every day less fathomable.* These words form between the poet and the child who has never seen her a mysterious kinship from which she will always feel excluded.

In the dead of night, Millicent wakes from the middle of a dream. In it, she was watching a woman she didn't know, long and white, and a little boy her own age – eight years old, perhaps, with blond curls and a smile on his lips – sitting silently on a cloud from which they were tearing off pieces to shape them like she does with salt dough that the cook sometimes makes for her to sculpt small animals from. Their creation done – dog, boat, whale – the woman and the child placed it in their open hands, blew on it, and let it go. They didn't speak to each other, but Millicent could sense between them such a deep complicity that, in her dream, her eyes welled up.

She throws back her sheets, gets up, and goes to the window. She doesn't know what time it is, but the moon, already high in the sky, almost full, gives off a milky light. Her father has explained to her a hundred times that the moon doesn't produce light but merely reflects, in the darkness, the fire of the sun. Millicent refuses to fully believe it. She is wary of mirrors.

The voices of her parents arguing rise up from downstairs. She can make out the names *Austin, Susan*. Her father sounds sad, and her mother exasperated. Sometimes it is the reverse; often both at the same time. She steps away from the window, crosses her bedroom on tiptoe, and pushes open the door, then she noiselessly goes down and leaves the house for the darkness of the garden. Homestead, nearby, is silhouetted against the sheet of the night like a shadow theatre. No matter where she goes, she feels like that house is always in her field of vision, like in paintings when the eyes of subjects seem to follow you wherever you go. The house will not stop watching her.

Suddenly she feels cold sting her cheek. Lifting her nose to the sky, she contemplates the clouds – dog, boat, whale – that glide past the moon. Snow is falling fine and lazy, like poplar pollen. With the tip of her finger, she takes the flake that has settled on her cheek, minuscule and perfect, with its six lacy branches, each one divided into symmetrical twigs, smaller and smaller, more and more miraculous. Nothing in the world could be more beautiful, in this very moment of this night in October 1886, in this exact place of Massachusetts, in the United States of America, than this first piece of white sky fallen to Earth.

Millicent stretches out on the frosted grass. She too feels like she is falling in the large basin of stars. On the pad of her finger, the snowflake doesn't melt. On the contrary: it burns; it is a tiny, white flame.

Last year, David taught his daughter to decipher the graduated numbers on the tube of the thermometer hanging in front of the window of the veranda. Every morning, as soon as she gets up, she goes to read the temperature, proudly announces the number for the day, and then records it in a notebook he gave her for this purpose.

She can tell you that on Christmas morning 1885, it was precisely 24 degrees on Mr. Fahrenheit's scale, or −4.4444 on that of Mr. Celsius. She still struggles to do the calculation necessary for the conversion but knows by heart the formula her father taught her: you take the temperature in degrees Fahrenheit, subtract 32, then divide by 1.8.

Her notebook is pristine, the numbers perfectly aligned, formed with a steady hand, not a day skipped. In flipping through the already filled pages, she is awed at all the days gone by and, contemplating the still-blank pages, all the mornings left to live.

Her morning notations have helped Millicent discover a passion. While her mother keeps a diary, writes articles, and composes music, and her father drafts scientific essays and strings together formulas, she makes lists, which are her way of organizing a world that is too vast and of which she knows virtually nothing. In a second notebook, the one bought with her pocket money, she records a list of her favourite months (*December, January, February, November*), a list of vegetables she hates (*turnip, salsify roots, cauliflower*), her favourite stars (*Sirius, Betelgeuse, Stella Maris, Venus,* which is not a star, but no matter), and the countries she dreams of visiting (all of them). A few pages later, there is the list of birds seen in a day, her favourite flowers, the colours she can make out in the nacre of a single oyster shell, the juiciest varieties of apples, the greatest qualities of dogs, her favourite adjectives, the noises in the night, writers she prefers above all others.

On a page titled *My best friends*, the lines have remained blank.

Things you can make with snow

Forts
Igloos
Snowballs
Snowmen
Angels

Everything is wonderfully quiet in the Dickinson home, which has more ghosts than living people. Thankfully, there are cats, who belong to both worlds at once. Lavinia sits in the parlour. The clock strikes ten; she has the day ahead of her. She often still feels the impulse, before starting any activity that will require a bit of time or leaving the house, to go check Mother's bedroom to see if she needs anything. But the bedroom is empty. All the bedrooms are empty, except her own. She doesn't have to worry about making honey porridge, or bringing a hard-boiled egg up to Emily, or going to the post office to mail one of the letters her sister continued to write, even in her final days, at a rate of several a week.

No one needs her anymore.

Slowly, she goes to the kitchen to put on her work apron, fills a bucket with water, arms herself with a brush and a bar of black soap, and starts scrubbing the steps of the large staircase one by one, as if polishing the keys of a giant piano.

Sometimes she wonders if they are all together. Are her father, her mother, her sister, and her nephew living up there in some heavenly home? If they are, who makes them dinner?

The sky above the treetops is felt grey. Lavinia dreams of sticking pins in it to prevent it from coming undone, breaking apart, long enough to climb a ladder and redo the seams. Every day of her life, she makes or repairs something. She embroiders, knits, darns, patches, mends, even does a little carpentry work. After lunch, she puts the finishing touches on a bonnet for the grandson of a childhood friend; all that is missing is the trim.

In the kitchen, an entire drawer is reserved for bits of ribbon, lengths of string, measures of lace. Unmatched buttons sit in a box: horn, leather, mother-of-pearl, wood, copper, iron; a jar holds remainders of thread and strands of wool, some of which are so short that she wonders from time to time, in searching through them, what they could be used for aside from weaving a robin's nest, but she doesn't throw anything out. The scraps of fabric are neatly laid out in a large box, like a quilt in pieces. A drawer contains a handful of keys; she can't remember what they open, but how do you throw away a key?

From among the tightly coiled ribbons, she chooses a pale yellow one twice as long as her hand, which will go nicely with the royal blue of the fabric, but one of its ends is lightly frayed. She opens a second drawer where the ends of candles are laid out. She places the ones that are really too short in a separate little bucket until she has enough to melt the wax to make fat tealights. She has to refrain from keeping the stems of burnt matches, sorry that she can't burn them twice.

She grabs the first candle, gently runs the base along the threads at the edge of the ribbon to prevent them from fraying more. Everything, no matter how insignificant, has its use. Nothing should be thrown away; it would be a sin not only of extravagance but also of lack of ingenuity.

Sometimes it seems to her that this leftover miscellany is what holds the house together; mysteriously, it is the mortar. If she were to get rid of the scraps of soap, pieces of chalk, trimmings of cardboard, remnants of fabric, ends of pencils, empty sugar and flour bags, only a hollow shell would remain.

It is no surprise that her sister wrote her poems on bits of envelope and packaging. Nothing is more solid than these remains; they are survivors, they are what endures when everything else has disappeared.

On the windowsill, in a saucer of water, a head of celery, a leek, and three green onions stubbornly grow in slow motion in the depths of winter, driven by an invisible force that she doesn't fully understand, which may be the light or may be the dogged faith of vegetables.

In the evening, Lavinia plucks from their stems lavender flowers that have been left to dry, and they fall in a fine, fragrant hail on the table. She slips a few spoonfuls into a sachet sewn from a remnant of striped poplin, which she closes with a string. She repeats until there are no flowers left. Her work done, she will slip the sachets in the closets and trunks, where they will fend off moths while perfuming the clothes. Out of habit, she has made far too many. Half the closets in the big house are now empty, three quarters of the bedrooms closed. Patiently, she empties the unneeded sachets in a bowl, goes out to the garden, and in the twilight throws the mauve flowers into the air to spread them like seeds to feed the birds. Nothing is wasted. For weeks to come, the chickadees will smell nice, like soap.

In a kitchen that in every way resembles that of Homestead – large, a waxed wood table, a six-burner stove, copper pots hanging from the ceiling with braids of garlic and strings of sage, tarragon, and bay leaves – Emily and Gilbert pour white sugar, brown sugar, and molasses in a pot, add a bit of water, vinegar, and cubes of butter that they handle with their fingers. They have flour in their hair and on the tips of their noses, like baker clowns. Laughing, they stir the mixture with a large wooden spoon. The taffy bubbles, turns dark blond, then caramel. They remove the pot from the heat, add white powder that must be baking soda, transfer the dough to a glass bowl where they let it cool a few moments. Then they each take hold of a ball as large as a grapefruit, pull on it, and fold it in time, forming long, increasingly thin and elastic strings that glisten between their fingers, until the taffy resembles liquid golden thread.

The scene has no smell, and that is how Lavinia knows she is dreaming.

And yet if asked, she would say that she never dreams. Truth be told, she doesn't believe in dreams; they are fantasies, fabrications from the imagination of minds more inventive or idle than her own. She vaguely suspects that some people make up dreams in the morning to appear interesting. She has no imagination, and she is no worse for it. Common sense, yes, resourcefulness, decidedly, the gift of talking to cats, of recognizing by instinct which, among a pyramid of melons, is the most fleshy and fragrant. This is ample compensation.

But for the past few weeks, her sister has been coming to her in her dreams. It is hardly surprising, when you think of it. Even in death, Emily has more than enough imagination for two.

No matter where she goes, Emily's ghost follows her, when she doesn't precede her. Diaphanous and evanescent in middle age, her sister has become the most lively of spectres.

Lavinia cannot bring herself to throw the herbarium on the fire as Emily had ordered for her personal papers, but she knows all too well, in turning the pages with their faded flowers, that she is entering the secret world of the departed more deeply than if she had read her diary. She feels like she is opening her gut to discover, where other people have innards and a heart, two massive lungworts, a purple liverwort, a large red peony.

&

In the morning, upon waking, Lavinia realizes that she hasn't bled in months. She tries to remember the last time. Was it May? June? When did she put her pads away? She doesn't know. This nest of flesh in her belly that formed and was undone and then ran between her legs every month, that warm flow has dried up. She will not have had children. She says the words out loud: 'I will not have had children,' struggling to understand this future perfect made up of a future and a past – when these two tenses collide, don't they cancel each other out? She grabs Ginger, who is winding between her ankles, brings her up to her face to bury her nose in the soft fur. Is it the sort of thing people generally regret? If Lavinia has a regret, it is that she hasn't had more cats.

Susan has long been wary of books, sensing that we wouldn't write if we didn't die. Books are a sign of death, like a lighthouse warns of a reef; in either case, it is a light we would rather do without. On the dull pages of volumes bound in animal skin, the dead speak to the living – and to other dead. Books are ghosts. Letters are not much better, made from the absence of someone we love. Even the most beautiful, the most tender, the most moving never stop whispering: *I'm not there.*

Emily's letters and poems pull Susan to both the day and the night, create in her nostalgia for a love that no longer exists, that maybe never existed. Because, past fifty, she knows that it is all well and good to search for the absolute in travel, in books, in faith, in morphine, in the arms of the one we think we love, or even in the starry sky, like that poor David, but it is only ever found in death. Some mornings, she is so tired when she opens her eyes that she feels like she is made from the same wood as her bed.

Popular wisdom has it that time eases sorrow, eventually dulls grief. That is not true, Susan thinks, it is just one more lie she has been told. Quite the opposite: every morning deepens her sorrow and sharpens her loss, and the hole in her chest grows larger; she could fall into it at any moment. She is not grieving only Emily and Gilbert. She is mourning her youth, her life half-consumed, half-disappointing, winter coming when she was just getting used to the fall.

Prostrated, huddled in her armchair, she has reached the age when one grows smaller. She thinks of the notches on the door frame where she and Austin marked the children's height every New Year's Day: Edward, long since taller than her, Martha, almost a woman already, Gib, who will forever remain at the height of her heart. If she had the whimsy to measure herself too, the notches would be diminishing, she is sure of it, counting back through everything that slips away from her, both within and without.

≥●

Days, then weeks pass. Susan is not working, Lavinia loses patience, goes to see her, asks for an update, leaves each time disappointed and vaguely irritated.

One morning, finally, while they are sitting in the parlour at Evergreens, Susan admits, 'I can't do it.'

'What?' Lavinia asks.

'Anything.'

She sweeps her hand, gesturing to the space around her, the parlour with the piano, her books, the house that surrounds her, the yard that contains it all, the town spread around it, the world beyond – useless, eccentric circles of an increasingly greater void.

Susan knows that there is no point trying to explain to Lavinia the hole deep in her chest, where what was most precious to her, most delicate and most alive, was ripped out of her. She continues to get up in the morning, to eat, even to laugh, sometimes, but her heart has predeceased her. It is lying under the earth at the cemetery; she is counting the days until she can join it. Yet words come out of her mouth, of their own volition, falling like little pebbles.

'I wake up in the morning, and my first thought is of Gib. He follows me, or I follow him, all day long. I talk to him out loud, I ask him what he wants to eat, if he needs something, whether he would like me to read to him. I go to bed at night praying I will join him in my sleep.'

Her voice cracks. Lavinia would like to put an arm around her sister-in-law's shoulders, but she knows that she would shrink from it. Her pain makes her too fragile for touch. At the slightest contact, she would shatter.

Susan has stopped looking at Lavinia; turned toward the window, she continues as if to herself.

'He must be so cold. For the past few days, I've been think-ing of nothing but. It is freezing at night, there is frost in the morning. His feet were always cold. He needed a hot water bottle every night.'

Lavinia picks up an armful of Emily poems. For the first time, Emily has failed to warm Susan.

When she returns the next day for the rest, Susan won't let her in. Lavinia lets a day go by, two, then a week. Through the closed door, she explains, argues, cajoles, then even conscripts Austin to try to convince Susan to return the rest of the manuscripts, all wasted breath. Susan refuses to lose Emily a second time.

Lavinia wonders whether the poems are like a deck of cards, and you need them all to win at solitaire. Before the closed door on the tenth day, after careful consideration, she decides it is not important that some are missing: winning be damned; they will just make them into a house.

Lavinia takes out her knitting needles, the softest yarn she can find, lambs wool with long, silky fibres, then sets to work. For three days, her needles tick and tock like a clock. In seeing the piece take shape from the ball of wool, she feels the satisfaction of a sculptor seeing emerge from a block of wood the bird, the house, the face held for all eternity in the secret of its grain. She regularly unwinds the wool, strings together stitches with quiet urgency, as you would read a text in which each word is necessary, inevitable, and yet uncertain. Each of these stitches is a loop snatched from chaos and formlessness, the link in a little chain that holds the living and the dead together.

Sunday, in the cemetery, after spending a moment in contemplation before Emily's gravestone, she takes the narrow path that leads to Gilbert's grave and sets on the ground the lambswool hat, scarf, and mittens that she knitted to keep him warm on November nights.

Millicent, who loves all books without exception, has a particular fondness for atlases. On their open pages, she likes to trace her finger along the sinewy line that marks the borders between countries and the courses of rivers. David shows her the route he travelled to witness the last eclipse he documented – half the planet.

She observes the large mass of Brazil, a country of fire, embers glowing under the sun; Chile, the bit at the end that stretches out, long like the chili of its name; Argentina, which she imagines as a country made of silver, *argentum*, where coins grow on trees, where river waters are golden, where the houses sparkle like jewels under a topaz sky; Ecuador, named for the fine line that encircles the planet. She quietly recites the city names that are also characters from stories: Montevideo the giant, Quito the dwarf, Córdoba the incorrigible rascal, Rosario the monk, Asunción, who is so irresistible that they are all in love with her, but the beauty has eyes only for Orion, who hunts invisible game high in the sky.

In particular she contemplates the vast expanses of blue that separate the continents. The lands seem to be set on water like figures on a game board, the pieces of a massive puzzle. On these oceanic realms that cover half the globe, there is no city, not the slightest inscription. Their wonders are invisible; they have not yet been discovered, spread out in the space between the names.

Her favourite territory is at the end of the long tongue of South America and bears the name *Tierra del Fuego, Terre de Feu, Land of Fire*, and she imagines it as a country in flames day and night, under the sun, the moon, and the eclipses.

She would like to go around the world in the footsteps of her father, who travels the planet to track comets, although she will look not to the sky but to the earth under her feet. She will gather a sample of each plant encountered, no matter how insignificant, even those without flowers, those adorned only with thorns; she will give them names, glue them in the herbarium that she started last summer and that remains tragically empty because nothing grows in their garden but roses and lilacs. She will make a second catalogue by sampling a handful of dirt each day that she will pour into a small jar, with the corresponding date and location – plenty of people collect dead butterflies, or coins or stamps, which have never been alive. She will observe this earth through a microscope; with a bit of luck, she will find in it the ash of extinct volcanos, the moraine of ancient glaciers, sand from rivers that have disappeared, shells of snails from large dried-up seas, the dust of stars her father claims the Earth is made from. To complete her collections, she will just have to figure out how to make a herbarium of raindrops and snowflakes.

❧

The little girl has been in bed for an hour, but sleep won't come. David, who went up to get a book, hears her tossing and turning under her sheets, and he cracks open the door. A dust-filled ray slides across the floor.

'If you aren't sleeping, do you want to get some air with me?'

Without hesitation, she leaps out of bed, puts her shawl around her shoulders, her slippers on her feet, and places her little footsteps in the large strides of her father as they go out into the garden. The night is like ink, but Millicent is not afraid of the dark.

'Did you know,' David asks, 'that some of the stars we see above our heads have been extinguished for years, even centuries?'

Millicent looks at him, dumbfounded, not knowing whether to believe him.

He explains. 'The light takes so long to reach us that a star can be dead by the time we finally see it.'

'Venus?' the little girl asks, worried.

'No. Venus is a planet. It can't go out, because it was never burning.'

'But how do you know which ones are dead?' Millicent asks.

'We don't know,' he admits, then he reaches for an image. 'They are ghost stars.'

She solemnly acquiesces. She herself, at this very moment, in a white nightgown, hair loose, big, shiny, dark eyes, looks like a little ghost who has fallen from the sky.

For months now, I have been walking in the footsteps of Millicent, Mabel, Susan, Lavinia. That could mean two things: that I am walking in their footsteps to follow their path, or that I exist, in some way, in all four of them. These two things are true at the same time. In each of these women, I have poured a bit of what I know, what I believe, what I fear, and what I am running from, and I have set them as cardinal points on a compass rose, hoping one of them will show me the path to take. But rather than staying sensibly put, they start shifting around, at first imperceptibly, then with a more confident step, moving away from or coming closer to each other, a dance that I didn't choreograph and to music I don't know. The fact that they hear it before me is reassuring: they are alive.

The path to take – it's a question Emily never would have asked, having known exactly where to go: nowhere. She had already arrived. She had never left.

> Going to Heaven!
> I don't know when –
> Pray do not ask me how!
> Indeed I'm too astonished
> To think of answering you!
> Going to Heaven!
> How dim it sounds!

And yet it will be done
As sure as flocks go home at night
Unto the Shepherd's arm!

Perhaps you're going too!
Who knows?
If you should get there first
Save just a little space for me
Close to the two I lost –
The smallest 'Robe' will fit me
And just a bit of 'Crown' –
For you know we do not mind our dress
When we are going home –

Lavinia is wearing her prettiest dress, pigeon blue, trimmed at the neck and cuffs with a very fine lace. It is a little tight at the waist, but no matter. Susan, Austin, Edward, and Martha are also in their Sunday best, as is the neighbour Mrs. Hansel, invited because she is a recent widow, and they don't want her to be alone. In the parlour of Evergreens stands a fir tree decorated with popcorn garlands and dried oranges slices – what a waste, Lavinia can't help but think, when marmalade is so easy to make.

They open the gifts, making the expected exclamations in discovering a print for one, a book for another, and for a third a pair of embroidered handkerchiefs. But their hearts aren't in it. Susan forces a smile for her two remaining children, even though they are no longer children. Christmas died along with Gilbert.

They set the table without enthusiasm.

'These oysters are delicious,' Mrs. Hansel says.

Lavinia makes a point of joining her and swallows three in a row. The champagne is growing warm in the flutes, everyone is picking at the plates in front of them, even though the turkey is perfectly done; what a shame, it will have been slaughtered for nothing. They light the pudding; it goes out smoking with the smell of suet. Then, at around 10 p.m., Austin announces that he needs air. Susan glares at him but doesn't say a word, and he leaves after putting on his coat and wrapping himself in a scarf.

'Why don't we play charades?' Martha suggests, and she and her brother take turns imitating famous characters, miming titles of books, feigning joy.

When Lavinia takes her leave a little before midnight, a light snow has started to fall. She lifts her face to the sky and takes a deep breath of cold air that burns her lungs, then starts walking at a brisk pace. In the distance, beyond the fence, she spots the shadow of Austin and the shadow of Mabel leaning toward each other, immobile, like statues. She wonders what David and Millicent are doing left alone on this Christmas night. She wonders, as she does almost every hour of every day, what Emily is doing.

When she sees a lark, Lavinia thinks of her sister alive. When she spots the red flash of a cardinal in the branches of the sycamore, she thinks of her sister. When she sees chickadees bustling, watches a starling on a roof, every time she hears a turtledove coo, as soon as a crow appears or a myna shimmers, Lavinia remembers Emily. All feathered creatures remind her of her sister – except maybe for chickens.

∂●

Between Christmas and the New Year, from the beginning of the afternoon, the rays pierce sidelong through the trees in the yard, transforming the few leaves still clinging to the branches into stained glass. Lavinia reflects that her dead sister's poems are the same: leaves shot through with light.

Standing in the garden in the middle of what remains of the squash and the pumpkins half-buried in the snow, she lifts her head, forces herself to look at the white sun in the blue sky without squinting. The brightness is dazzling: a dull pain. The light bores a hole in her eye, to the back of her skull. Tears run down her cheeks, but she does not blink. Black dots start dancing in front of her, bigger and bigger, more and more of them. They cover her field of vision like ink splotches running together into one. For a moment she is sure she has lost her sight – which is to say that perhaps she will finally see. When she closes her eyes, this other darkness is like cool water. If too much light makes you blind, what happens when you suffer from too much love?

She goes back inside, and the cats immediately come to curl up against her. They arrive one by one, walking regally, flop on their sides, and start purring in unison: Ginger in the crook of her knees, Cinnamon hugging the curve of her shoulder, Pepper against the small of her back.

Her body ends precisely where their soft fur begins. If they were all to get up at once, she might come apart, spill out; she is afraid she would never get back up. She would remain there, a bundle of loose-jointed limbs, a puppet in its box, waiting to be assembled. In the depths of winter, the warmth of the cats will hold her together.

From time to time, Lavinia takes Emily's herbarium from the large box where she has stored it, and she flips through it as she would a printed book, always stopping on the same pages to admire the delicate balance of the composition, the slim stems, the colours that are starting to fade while the outlines of the plants remain clear. She is particularly fascinated by the white space between the flowers. Her sister had a talent for setting living things in a sort of eternity. Lavinia had long quietly envied this gift that filled with wonder all those whom Emily rewarded with her poems, letters, or even her razor-sharp repartee.

The herbarium closed, she goes down to the kitchen, takes from the cold room the jar in which the sourdough she has been feeding for two decades is macerating. She adds a bit of water, a spoonful of flour to the mixture, stirs, and puts the jar back in the cold. She will come back later to prepare tomorrow's bread. Not for a second does she think about this equal, if not greater, miracle, through which she is creating life from dead things.

At the start of the new year, Emily's poems under her arm, Lavinia goes to see the man her sister, in the dozens of letters she wrote him, called her mentor. Thomas Higginson half stands to receive her. Writer, journalist, literary critic, an early abolitionist, he is an accomplished man, pleasing in appearance, and he knows it. His workroom looks like the one Father had at home: walls with walnut panelling, half of which are covered with bookshelves; a single window through which a tree, frozen like a painting in its frame, can be seen; an imposing desk that seems to signify the grandeur of the task he devotes himself to.

That is where Lavinia unceremoniously sets down the suitcase she has brought with her. He raises his bushy eyebrows. She unbuckles the straps, fiddles with hardware, and lifts the flap. Inside are jumbled tens, hundreds, of sheets, scraps of paper, corners of envelopes covered with the handwriting he knows so well. For a moment it takes his breath away.

'My sister left poems,' Lavinia announces tersely.

It is an effort for him to start breathing again; he picks up a sheet, then another, scrambles to decipher a few words. It's not a poem, not exactly, a draft, perhaps, something like the shadow, the memory, or the promise of a poem. Elsewhere, a paper has a single verse in the middle of which a word is stroked out; below, a series of terms that seem synonymous but aren't. After years of knowing her only through her letters, he feels he is finally entering Emily Dickinson's bedroom.

'I want to have them printed,' Lavinia continues.

He nods, takes another scrap of paper, seven words, then another, a stanza – but is it indeed a stanza if the four lines are of irregular length and don't rhyme? He collects himself.

'My dear madam … ' he begins, then, 'Lavinia, may I call you Lavinia?'

He can call her Esmerelda for all she cares; she just wants him to print her sister's poems. He who has this quasi-magical power, she wants him to transform them into a book.

'My dear Lavinia, these … these writings cannot be printed in this state. And are they even really poems?' (Here, he brandishes a scrap of paper with three lines, the last one almost illegible.) 'Regardless, they have to be deciphered, then transcribed, edited, revised, proofread, all processes that require patience, rigour, and meticulousness. You are not unaware of my professional obligations; it would take months, years perhaps, to see this through.'

Something suddenly seems to occur to him, and he thinks out loud.

' … unless … unless you find someone who would agree to perform this preliminary task, in which case it would be my pleasure to present the manuscript to a publisher. I know several who would no doubt accept this sort of project on my recommendation – because as you know I have the good fortune of enjoying a modest reputation in our small literary world ...'

His smile contradicts this false humility, which Lavinia thinks suits him like a top hat on a porcupine. She closes the suitcase abruptly, takes her leave, sets off with her sister's book in a thousand pieces in her cardboard suitcase.

Back at Homestead, she goes up to Emily's bedroom and sets the suitcase on the bed. Not knowing what to do anymore, she has an impulse that has not come to her in years: asking Austin's advice. Of the Dickinson household, they are the only ones remaining. Gift or burden, don't these poems belong as much to him as to her?

'And did he suggest someone?' Mabel asks Austin a few hours later, after he talked with Lavinia about it.

They are walking together, one metre apart as dictated by decorum, but from time to time, Austin stretches his arm toward Mabel and she places her small palm in the large hand and withdraws it just as quickly, a bird lifting off.

'No, I don't think so. And trust me, it won't be easy to find the right person for the job.'

'How true,' Mabel agrees with a nod. She never disagrees with him. 'First, it needs to be someone who knew dear Emily a little.'

'Exactly.'

'But it is not sufficient to have known her. That person also has to have a strong literary sensibility.'

'Precisely.'

'Perhaps not a professor though, or a publisher, or a critic ...'

'No?'

'Perhaps instead someone who is not otherwise occupied and who can devote themselves to this monumental task, don't you think?'

'Of course.'

This is what he would have pointed out to Lavinia, if he had had time. His ideas are much clearer now. Truly, walking is salutary for putting order to one's thoughts.

'But who, who in Amherst could handle it?' Mabel asks. 'Yes, who?'

Mabel thinks out loud. 'Publishers and professors won't have the time, you're right there ... But then ... Maybe ... a woman?'

Austin starts but doesn't say a word. Their walk is nearing its end. They have to say goodbye until evening; he will come to knock on the door of The Dell once Millicent is in bed (David is on watch at the observatory) for a final sweet, a little slice of heaven after dinner, as she so prettily put it the other day. If he didn't hold himself back, he would devour her pink cheeks soft as peaches right here, her cherry lips, her hair fragrant with nutmeg.

'I know you'll be able to find the right person,' Mabel adds, her hazelnut eyes looking deep into those of Austin. 'The solution to the thorniest problem is sometimes right under our nose.'

She walks away with her lively step, looks back after a few metres, certain he is still watching her. She is not wrong.

That evening, Austin returns to Evergreens after midnight. He pushes open the door and goes up the stairs on tiptoe, so as not to wake his wife and children. He undresses, performs his ablutions, regretting he has to wash off the smell of his beloved, then slips under the duvet with a book. An hour goes by before he puts out his lamp. It takes him a while longer to fall asleep. He tosses and turns under the covers trying to get comfortable, his legs restless. The matter of Emily's poems is bothering him. He feels as though the solution is within reach, but it slips away as soon as he approaches. Mabel's face, her fine silhouette, her mischievous smile get tangled in his thoughts, and he tries feebly to chase them off to think about the problem at hand. And then Emily's and Mabel's faces come together in his mind, like two strangers colliding in a train station concourse, and from this encounter light emerges: it is, of course, Mabel to whom he should entrust Emily's poems.

When, for the first time, Lavinia enters the Todds' home, she is not intimidated, albeit slightly uncomfortable; she feels like she is suddenly entering a foreign dominion where she doesn't know the customs. The parlour, which is not very big, is decorated with taste and flair.

Mabel serves tea with her pale hands, and does it gracefully, like everything else.

Lavinia squirms on the sofa covered with silky fabric in gold and red flowers.

'Did you paint these?' she asks the young woman.

Austin had told her, with admiration, that Mabel sometimes hand-painted fabric with patterns so well executed that you would have thought they were from Liberty.

Mabel bursts into tinkling laughter.

'Goodness me, no! That would have taken me months! I content myself with more modest projects: handkerchiefs, scarves, the occasional blouse …'

Lavinia nods. The tea is perfect: hot but not scalding, lightly spiced, with floral notes. She looks around at the prints, the knick-knacks, the revolving globe on a stand, down to the Persian carpet that covers the middle of the floor. A few natural curiosities are exhibited in a glass cabinet: the brightly coloured shell of a turtle, an ostrich egg, a geode the green crust of which hides a sparkling interior, and a curious elongated, pale object, which seems made of tens of fine, regularly spaced rings.

Mabel has followed her gaze. 'It's a snake skeleton,' she explains, before her guest can ask the question.

Lavinia nods, as if nothing could be more normal. She takes another sip and then dives in. 'You no doubt know that for the past few months I have been gathering my sister's poems together to make a book.'

Mabel nods without speaking, but her attention is complete, almost palpable.

'And, truth be told, the work has not advanced as quickly as I would have hoped ... '

She does not dare mention Susan; it would have been a sort of impropriety. But the fact is that Susan was unable to do anything for weeks other than read and reread the pages that Lavinia entrusted to her, as if Emily had hidden in them some secret that would be revealed only through erosion.

Mabel nods again. She already knows, through Austin, that the work has amounted to nothing. She smiles at Lavinia to encourage her to go on. But she does not seem to know what she has come to ask for: advice, help, simply an outside opinion?

Lavinia stammers, 'Yes, um well ... I wanted ... We tried ... It seems to me that ... '

Mabel interrupts her, unable to contain herself any longer. 'But of course, Lavinia. I would be delighted, *delighted*, to do the editing.'

There, it is settled. Without Lavinia having to ask the question. She wants to take a last mouthful of tea, but it has cooled and its aromas have dissipated. It is like drinking tepid water.

Mabel has always dreamed of making a book. She tried her hand at the genres normally reserved for girls: occasional poetry, speeches, short texts extolling the charms of nature, which unfortunately does not awaken any particular emotion in her, as she far prefers the bustle of the city to the death-like calm of the country. She has composed sketches, verse, ditties. She has written a few reviews of novels and poetry collections, two or three expositions on philosophical questions that particularly interested her because they allowed her to show off the subtleties of her mind. But all these attempts left her unsatisfied. The result was never worthy of the insight she knew she possessed but that seemed to fade as soon as she put words on the page. She can't find the instrument she needs.

At birth, the fairies leaned over her cradle to shower her with gifts: pretty features, a lively mind, a sense of repartee, a clear voice, and agile fingers on the ivory keys, curiosity, confidence in her abilities, a velvety gaze that she knows drives men wild, a supple waist, and a light step, all things that make one shine in society and that one is bored with when alone; and then, in her breast, a hole impossible to fill.

Emily was a star burning all alone in her bedroom; Mabel flames and goes out a hundred times a day, like a candle that is lit and extinguished, and that produces light that is reflected only in the gaze of others. The greater the gaze, the more majestic she becomes.

In a letter to David, one year before their marriage, she had written: *Do you think I will be satisfied with myself once I am an extraordinary musician, & a talented painter, & a brilliant student of French, German, Latin, & Greek, & an astronomer, botanist, ornithologist, & mythologist, and master of literature in general?*

A question with so many parts can have but one answer: no.

Mabel is so attached to the idea of making a book because she still can't settle for just one life. She needs to believe that other existences are possible, all at once, that she is not forced to make a choice and stick to it forever, that several chances are given to her again and again, every day, every hour of her life. Literature, as she sees it, is the opposite of this self-denial.

And so, all the imagination she might have devoted to inventing that book, she has so far used to invent herself. But she has finally been given the instrument she was missing: another's voice, thanks to which she will be able to publish a volume of poetry, without equal or rival, an utterly new and original work, of which she will be not the author, but, even better, because it is more powerful, more detached, freer, the editor.

Without her, this book would not exist; there would be just scraps of paper smelling of spices, mildewing in the bottom of a drawer. She will turn these fragments into a book, a miracle as great as turning water to wine.

In the massive forest Millicent explores, the ground is carpeted with last fall's oak leaves, like singed parchment. The acorns hide in them by the hundreds, clandestine, and together dream of becoming a new forest, bigger, more abundant, with leaves brandished up high, like flags. All except one, the smallest, the least round, the one whose skin is the finest, the same caramel as the leather of the stillborn calf that vellum is made from. It does not dream of becoming an oak; it wants to be a reed.

The poplar leaves that have survived the winter are silent coins that tumble in the wind. Money grows on trees. Better than money: birds and squirrels too.

The pine needles smell like Christmas; she could just close her eyes and reach out to pick an orange pitted with cloves. Buried among the twigs and dead leaves, the clusters of mushrooms are coffee-coloured villages that contain tiny stories. Not far off, a giant's flute tries to pass itself off as a large dead tree that is still standing, pierced with holes at regular intervals by a woodpecker. There is nothing for it: whatever she does, Millicent is always too big or too small. The sun drops among the branches to play hide-and-seek with her. She greets it with a wink, and it responds in kind.

When she goes back in the house, twigs in her hair, knees scuffed with soil, a snag in her skirt, her mother cries: 'Good heavens, where have you been? We've been waiting for you for tea; your father has been worried sick!'

'I was in the forest.'

'The forest? What forest?'

Millicent points to the small wooded area that borders the land: three oaks, four birches, a handful of pines.

∂❧

In the evening, at nightfall, David and Millicent go out into the yard and he says, 'Look, tell me what you see.'

She lifts her nose toward the swarm milling over their heads. 'Stars. Lots of stars. And planets.'

'That's right. And the moon?'

She looks to the left, to the right, then remarks, 'It's not there.'

'You're right. We can't see it tonight. This phase is called the *new moon.*'

Millicent had always thought that the new moon was the crescent she waited to see appear through her bedroom window, fine as a thread in the immense sky. 'But why *new* if we can't see it?'

David never mocks her ignorance. He answers patiently. 'Because it marks the start of a new cycle. In the coming days, it will gradually appear, first a quarter, then it will be gibbous, and then full, then it will slowly disappear during the second half of the month. But you are not the only one who finds the name strange; some prefer to call it the *dark moon.*'

Around them, crickets and frogs sing their metallic song, which comes from everywhere all at once, a second swarm milling. Millicent tries to guess where in the sky the invisible moon is floating.

'You know what's special about this phase?' David asks.

'No.'

'It's during this period that the moon is between the sun and the earth, so it is at that moment, and only at that moment, that solar eclipses occur.'

Her father knows all the mysteries of the sky and teaches them to her one by one, like letters in an expansive alphabet. The two of them string together the Little Dipper, Pegasus, Draco, Lynx, far-off and formidable creatures, and Millicent thinks about this miracle: invisible, the ash-covered rock manages to eclipse the flaming star. In the space of an instant, night triumphs in the middle of the day. All is not lost for her, she who is just as small and dark.

Upon waking, Lavinia goes down to the kitchen, puts on the water for tea, opens the door, and the cats rush inside. One by one, they come to set their offerings from the night at her feet: a tiny field mouse, its frozen legs tucked as if it were pulling an invisible sheet up under its chin; a baby bird that fell from the nest, its bulging eyes visible through its closed eyelids; a dragonfly with stained-glass wings; a long pine cone. Then, tails in the air, they proudly head toward the saucers of milk she has set on the floor for them. She gently grumbles at them for being such able hunters, a reproach they take as congratulations.

After her breakfast – the same one for years: a soft-boiled egg, a slice of bread, berry jam, a cup of tea – she wraps the mouse, the baby bird, and the dragonfly in a clean handkerchief, goes to the back of the garden to dig three shallow holes, barely the length of her foot, places in each one the tiny remains, which she covers with earth. Then she takes three strawberry plants she has sprouted in the kitchen from achenes, which are waiting to be placed in the earth, and plants them alongside some twenty similar little mounds – raspberries, blackberries, elderberries. In summer, her cemetery will become a fruit garden. In the fall, jam for the winter.

જી

It is time to transplant the rest of the seedlings that have grown from these tiny lives that slept all winter and that must be buried to awaken. Like every year, she put the seeds in soil in mid-March, when the nights were still cold, like performing a magical rite: how, from such a small thing, can a whole plant spring forth, with its stem, flowers, pods, fruit, and new seeds? Our Lord, it seems, fed five thousand men with five loaves of bread and two fish. Lavinia has never understood the mysteries of the gospel, but if she is given five seeds and enough time, she too could feed five thousand famished people.

She steps into the greenhouse where for years her mother and then her sister grew orchids, and she sets her seedlings in the middle of the flowers that have survived. She has asked the maid to go in only once a week to trim and water them, as if to avoid disrupting the rest of the creatures plunged deep in sleep. When she crosses the threshold, the cats follow her: suspicious, they sniff the air, then walk ahead of her, stretch out purring in the sun pouring through the glass wall that runs almost floor to ceiling.

The sleeping flowers all look alike. It requires an immense effort of imagination to picture that they have been luxuriant, perfumed creatures and that they may become that again: for the moment, they are a small forest of twigs as dry as the stakes that prop them up. It is impossible to say which are dead and which are preparing to make new buds. Lavinia has never understood anything about orchids, or roses, or lilies, or all the fragile, capricious creatures Emily cultivated. She has always been more comfortable kneeling in the cabbage patch or the pumpkin corner, among the tendrils of beans, the potent smell of tomato plants, or with fingers in the humus in search of clumps of potatoes – all plants she understands the purpose of, which she can dice, season, and cook in a stew.

This morning, she nonetheless puts aside the stems she is reasonably sure will not reflower and sparingly waters the others; she doesn't dare talk to them as her sister did, since she does not speak their language. When she leaves without accomplishing much, the cats remain, stretched out on the black and white tiles.

The next day, Austin, who has come for news, glances in the greenhouse through the half-open door. Seeing the desolate room, the empty pots, the plants bare of flowers, the place abandoned to cats, he can't help but remark, 'What a pity.'

Lavinia replies without turning, 'Not at all, you can see full well that I'm growing cats.'

As she is digging up earth to receive the pepper and tomato plants, Lavinia discovers shards of blue and white crockery. She stops, dumbstruck, as if she has exhumed the remains of an incredible ancient city, then she remembers the evening her sister, tired of Father's reprimands for always setting a chipped plate before him, calmly went to shatter it in the garden. She even remembers what they had eaten that night – rabbit in mustard sauce, cabbage, beets, potatoes – and again sees Emily come back in, dignified, and sit back down at the table without anyone daring to say a word.

Kneeling, she roots around in the soil for other pieces, which she places one by one in her handkerchief. Susan had come to knock at the door, and not receiving an answer, had walked around the house to find her digging in the soil with her nails.

'Sweet Jesus, what are you doing?'

Lavinia looks up, shows her the shards. Susan frowns, wants to ask another question, but chooses instead to kneel next to her, roll up her sleeves, and start digging furiously too, exclaiming when she feels a piece of porcelain under her fingers. Once they have turned the soil over twice, they go back in to wash their hands, and Lavinia puts the shards in a bowl of clean water. Using a brush and a small piece of soap, they wash them, carefully polish them, then dry them one by one before placing them on the kitchen table like pieces of a puzzle. Some almost assemble themselves. Some seem to go with no others.

'What was it?'

'A plate.'

With her hands, Lavinia indicates a disc the size of a watermelon. On the table, the round form is pierced with gaping holes. There are missing pieces of the puzzle. There is enough to make a saucer, a very small bowl in a pinch, but not a plate. What happened to the other pieces – did they disintegrate over the years, did the garden soil swallow them, is there, unbeknownst to them, growing somewhere in the yard a plant with tiny white and blue porcelain blooms?

Susan gives up first. 'We'll never do it. There are too many missing pieces.'

Lavinia doesn't let herself get discouraged. She shrinks the circumference of her circle, moves the pieces, tries to match others that clearly don't go together. Then she too stops.

'We could always glue this section back together,' Susan suggests, indicating a half dozen pieces that more or less fit together. 'It would be better than nothing.'

But Lavinia scoops up all the pieces but one, puts them in the handkerchief and ties the corners, and goes back out to bury them at the base of an apple tree.

When she comes back in, she takes from the cupboard the heavy pestle she uses to grind spices, and, with a slow, deliberate gesture, smashes the shard that remains on the table into smaller fragments. Susan startles and stares at her, dumbfounded. Lavinia chooses one of the pieces, which is the shape of a thin crescent moon, and slips it into the locket she wears around her neck; she holds out a vaguely triangular piece to Susan, then she puts on the water for tea.

'Sometimes,' she remarks, measuring out the leaves that she pours into the teapot, 'we try to repair things when we really need to find a way to break them better.'

When she thinks of Emily, Gilbert, or her cousin Sophia, who died at age fifteen, Lavinia sees them as they were in the spring or summer of their lives, carefree as puppies. But she knows that the truth is entirely different, more marvellous still; their fragile flesh has broken down, their bones are as smooth as piano keys, their hair is like spider silk, their hearts, their lungs, the whites of their eyes, and the pink flesh of their fingers have returned to the earth; they are feeding the tender grass; they have become willow, linden, sycamore; they are used as homes for birds, and their wide-open arms finally touch the stars in the sky.

In the garden, at nightfall, the fireflies trace moving garlands that dance for a moment and are immediately undone. Lavinia watches them from the kitchen window, stops the cats from going out so as not to bother the fairies. When she goes upstairs, hours later, passing by Emily's bedroom, the door of which is ajar, she discovers that a firefly, just one, has got into the house and is blinking above the pillow.

Mabel has decided that Millicent needs friends her own age, so Mrs. Hutchison's two daughters, aged eight and ten, with their blond ringlets, come to spend the afternoon at The Dell. They look over Millicent's bedroom with a merciless eye.

'You don't have many toys,' says the older sister, who is named Constance.

'Or dolls,' adds the younger one, named Faith.

'All you have is books,' the eldest continues, appalled.

To soften their disappointment, Millicent takes from her desk the kaleidoscope that Mr. Dickinson gave her and offers it to Faith.

'If you look inside, it's like magic.'

The younger one presses her eye to the opening, turns the ring a few times, passes the instrument to her older sister, who is soon bored with it too.

'Do you at least have a game of Parcheesi?' she asks.

'No.'

'Checkers?'

'No.'

The two sisters tap their feet. The little sister sits on the floor and sulks. The older one, arms crossed, glares at Millicent, who, backed into a corner, goes to her bookshelf, takes out two of her favourite volumes, a dictionary and an encyclopedia of fish, and presents one to each of them. This occupies them for a few minutes. As for Millicent, she is plunged into an adventure novel so fast-paced that she has soon forgotten the presence of her guests and jumps when Constance coughs. Constance absently places her book on the floor, and asks in a cheery voice, 'Why don't we play hide-and-seek?'

'Oh, yes!' her sister exclaims, and Millicent has no choice but to go along.

'You count,' Constance commands her.

Millicent closes her eyes, puts her fists to her ears, and starts a slow countdown, beginning at fifty. The world ceases to exist; all she can hear is the sound of her own voice and the blood pulsing in her eardrums like the ocean in a shell. She intentionally stretches the interval that separates each number from the next, as if to never reach zero, to never have to open her eyes.

Even so, she ends up announcing, almost regretfully, 'Ready or not, here I come!'

First, she looks under the bed. No one. The wardrobe: nothing. She takes a moment to part the clothes in the closet to ensure the little girls are not hiding between two dresses. There is no trace of them behind the door. Nor between the curtain and the wall. That is when, through the window, she spots the sisters fleeing as fast as their legs will carry them, laughing, their skirts swirling around their knees, their curls light in the wind.

Millicent sighs, picks up the fish encyclopedia abandoned on the floor, opens it to the narwhal page, the most solitary of unicorns.

When, later, she goes out into the forest that her mother insists on calling 'the little woods,' Millicent discovers on a trunk stripped of its bark a complicated line, a map written in a foreign language, a small labyrinth that she tries to decipher by following it with her finger, as those who cannot see do to decode the books transcribed in the writing invented by Mr. Braille. If only she knew better how to read them, these dozens of branching trails would tell her the story of the tree and of the forest. They might also give her the formula to sing better, be more graceful, make friends other than in books, be more like her mother.

Mabel, Lavinia, and Higginson all meet for the first time. While Lavinia had pictured herself as the client, expressing her wishes, preferences, and desires, she soon finds herself listening to Higginson, who seats Mabel and her on the other side of the massive desk from which he presides.

'Of course,' he says straight off, 'certain adjustments must be made.'

'Of course,' Mabel agrees.

'Like what?' Lavinia asks.

'Well, let's take the matter of the dashes, for example. There are far too many, obviously. They lose their impact. Plus, they disrupt reading, hinder the movement of thought. It is a completely understandable mannerism in an unpublished poet, but it is our duty, as editors, to clarify expression.'

'Excuse me,' Lavinia interjects. 'I'm not an expert on poetry, or editing ...'

'Decidedly,' Higginson confirms.

'I'm not an expert on these matters, but I know my sister. If Emily had wanted her expression to be clear, it would have been.'

The sentence is flimsy, she can feel it, as is her thought: she seems to be saying that her sister should have been clear. She is not used to discussing things that can't be touched with a finger or tasted with a tongue, lofty, abstract things, particularly with an authority of Mr. Thomas Higginson's stature. Powerless, she turns to Mabel for help. But the young woman, sitting erect with her hands folded in her lap, all smiles, has eyes only for the editor.

Lavinia keeps limping along. 'If Emily put the dashes there, it is because they meant something for her, don't you think?'

'Very well,' he retorts, in a tone reserved for young children and the simple-minded. 'What do you think they mean?'

Lavinia is caught short. 'I don't know,' she stammers, 'but the fact that I don't know doesn't mean she didn't know. Maybe … maybe they are part of Emily's language.'

Higginson can't help but laugh, and Mabel does likewise, taking care to half hide her smile behind a gloved hand.

'Emily's language, what a thought. If you will agree, my dear ladies, we shall publish these poems in the English language.'

It's hopeless, and she knows it. But Lavinia will not admit defeat. 'I don't know what all the beams and struts in a barn or a house are for. But it would never occur to me to remove some at random, out of fear that the whole building would collapse.'

Higginson stops laughing, but Mabel is the one who speaks. 'My dear Lavinia, it is not a question of changing the meaning or, for the most part, the form of the poems, but simply of making them more legible, more grammatically correct. Trust us.'

Lavinia suddenly feels exhausted. She would like to say that, from what she understands, her sister's poetry is the opposite of correct; that it belongs to the realm of the error, of that which does not appear in textbooks or dictionaries; that it resides quite apart from the usual, the expected; that the poetry lives in that surprise, that it is built from astonishment like the hive is built from honey. Emily's poems are the opposite of a straight line – labyrinth, bee's flight – at the same time as they go straight to their mark, like an arrow to its target, that they are at once the arrow, the target, the hand that shoots, and the air split by the steel tip.

She would like to say all this but doesn't know where to start. She ends up getting up, followed by Mabel, and wondering for the first time if it wouldn't have been better to throw her sister's poems in the fire, which would have taken them as they were.

Watching Austin chew every mouthful of leg of lamb twenty times before swallowing, studying his high forehead lined with three horizontal wrinkles that express constant worry, Susan can't find the young man of twenty who made her heart race. She remembers the excitement of the morning of her nuptials with something close to astonishment, as the memory seems to belong to a stranger. She recalls her agitation every time she entered the Dickinson household, her clammy hands, the butterflies in the pit of her stomach. On the periphery of these memories, like an object that flits at the edge of our field of vision but that we know we won't see at all if we give in to the temptation of turning our head to look at it dead on, Emily's silhouette.

She contemplates her life the way one would stop at the top of a hill after a long walk to survey the path travelled. She is struck by an idea that she can never clearly put into words but that has been haunting her increasingly in recent years: once travelled, this path takes on an unavoidable, necessary character, as if it had always been the only one possible. And yet, at every moment of our lives, ten, twenty paths are available, with little to distinguish them, all equally improbable, risky, uncertain. What if she had not married Austin, but instead his friend Nathan, a doctor, who did not lose a son?

What if instead she had chosen to hitch her destiny to that of Graham, who left Amherst for Paris (Paris!), where he teaches literature and translates French poets. What if she had married no one – if she had continued to write, like Emily, who saw talent in her? Which Susan would she have become? Passing her in the street, would she recognize the woman she sees in the mirror? She remembers the mazes in the magazines of her childhood, where she tried, tracing with her finger, all the paths, starting at the centre to reach the exit, backtracking when she found herself at an impasse. Life doesn't allow us to retrace our steps; it condemns us to advancing – or remaining immobile. Once stopped, how much time does it take to no longer feel one's arms and legs, Susan wonders. How many years before finally turning into a statue or a tree?

She spends the evening with her friend's letters, fanned out so she can embrace them with her eyes. In truth, it is Emily who is spread out, displayed, unfurled around her. She is in a thousand pieces. She is every age all at once.

In a letter dating back many years, she reads:

I see thee better in the dark,
I do not need a light.

One by one, Susan turns out the lights until she finds herself in the dark. She waits until her eyes adjust, until they learn to make out the shadows.

In my reading and research about pilgrimage sites to write *The Island of Books*, something obvious struck me: Mont-Saint-Michel, Santiago de Compostella, Lourdes, and Lisieux are not the end of the journey, but simply mark the middle. Once you have arrived at the site that had been the goal, you have to turn around and go back, whether home or somewhere else – unless you choose one of two possibilities on either end of the spectrum: you become a monk, or you keep walking forever. How is it that in the pilgrims' stories, journals, and other accounts, they talk only about the journey there, and never the return? Is that voyage of such little interest because it brings us back to the known and seems the opposite of exploration, like a renouncement, even denial? Do we ever emerge from a maze by retracing our steps? What if the real journey starts on the first day of the return trip – or even the very last, when we open our front door and set down our bags?

Pilgrimages, forests, books, our lives: all mazes.

The Maze: A Labyrinthine Compendium, reads: 'If the maze is a metaphor for life [...], the "goal" of the maze is not its centre. The middle of the journey of life, as Dante notes in "Inferno," the first part of *The Divine Comedy*, is the moment we get lost.'

The maze whose description inspired this explanation, the Altjeßnitz, in Germany, dates back to 1730 and is unique because it was made using hornbeam bushes (in French, also known as *charme*, or charm). But while the hornbeam has exceptionally hard wood, it does not have long life, a scant century at the most. This means that four generations of hornbeams have had to succeed each other, like four spells, for the maze to survive.

The same question of the midpoint and the half, although in a different form: in the eighteenth century, Carl Linnaeus, the father of botany, invented a garden that was a clock, which would tell the time with flowers. The plants were carefully chosen based on when they bloom and close; four o'clocks, which open their petals at dawn, followed by evening primrose, the scarlet pimpernel, then the dandelion, and so on, until the end of the day, at around five o'clock, when the chicory folds its corolla for the night. In observing which of the flowers was open, we would know the approximate time of day (by looking at the position of the sun in the sky above the garden too, no doubt, but that is not the point).

However, what these flowers had in common was that they were all diurnal; Linné's floral clock was good for only half the day. How would the night be measured?

How is a life measured? How do we weigh it? Where is the heavenly scale the Holy Scriptures speak of?

Is it counted in children brought into the world, in books written or published? In pies baked, successful cakes, socks knit? In beings lost, found, saved? In countries visited, territories explored? In fires lit – or extinguished? In letters written, received, never sent? In a few words chiselled on a gravestone? In a memory left with the living (but what then, when the living in turn reach the realm of the dead and the memory of the memory has disappeared)? In houses built, money earned, spent, dispersed? In good done, services rendered? In cats collected? In baby birds rescued? In plates shattered or glued back together? In honours received, medals pinned, jobs held? In books read, lent, dreamed of, never published? In flowers cultivated, trees planted, fruit picked?

And what if Lavinia, not content just to burn Emily's letters, had committed her sister's poems to the flames? Can a life be measured in poems, as one would count the syllables in an alexandrine?

Millicent goes down on tiptoe so as not to attract attention. She wants to surprise her mother; she has even
done her braids for the night, with all the care in the world,
tugging on the three interlaced sections of hair until they were
as stiff, solid, and shiny as barley sugar, then she chose her
prettiest ribbon, took two tries to make a nice, puffy periwinkle
bow at the end of each braid. Mabel rarely works this late,
but she has to show Mr. Higginson an initial selection of texts
in a few days, and her anxiety is palpable.

The dining room is the only room where they have
bothered to light the lamps. It is as if the golden glow is rising
from the accumulated poems to light Mabel's face as she sits
at the table piled with scraps of paper all in hues of white:
egg, cream, porcelain, ivory, goose, snow. Some have a hint of
blue, grey, or yellow; they seem old, so brittle that they could
turn to dust between their fingers. In any event, Mabel handles
them with great care. She holds one in front of her, squints,
and on a separate paper, she jots down a few words, scratches
them out, squints some more, as if what she is trying to
decipher is so small that she needs a tiny window to thread
the words through.

Millicent comes a few steps closer.

'Hello, my love,' her mother says, without looking up, as
she takes a sip of tea – she always works with a little teapot

beside her filled with a very dark, floral, sweet liquid, which Millicent likes the smell of so much she would like to make perfume out of it.

The little girl draws a deep breath. David steps into the dining room, and Mabel speaks to him.

'Take a look at this,' she says, holding out the paper she is recopying.

He sits down. He squints. He reads in a soft voice, making it out as he goes:

> *The Grass so little has to do*
> *A sphere of simple Green*
> *With only Butterflies to brood*
> *And bees to entertain.*

Millicent reaches out to take the half-torn paper with pointy little letters that make her think of little bird tracks in the snow.

'Don't touch,' Mabel says, not looking at her. Then to David, she says, 'Skip to the end.'

> *'The Grass so little has to do / I wish I were Hay.'*

He doesn't have time to finish before Mabel says, 'No, precisely.'

'No, what?'

'Look, there's an *a*. She wrote *I wish I were a Hay.'*

He can't help but laugh a little.

'She was distracted. She made a mistake. No one says *a hay.'*

Millicent thinks. It's true, there is no such thing as *a hay*. But she thought that's what books were for, to write what doesn't exist. Without looking, she takes the scrap of paper closest to her.

'Precisely.'

Mabel appears to suddenly become aware of the time.

'Go upstairs, Millicent, and get to bed,' she says, touching her shoulder in a manner that is part caress, part dismissal.

Millicent could have cut her hair in a bowl cut and her mother wouldn't have noticed. Maybe she will do it one day. She clutches the scrap of paper in her closed fist, like a talisman, then starts up the large staircase with this little light in her hand.

That night, Millicent is not alone in her bedroom; she has found a friend. Better yet, she has invented her, and the friend has invented her in return. Millicent reads the few words written by Emily, and the enclosures of her bedroom collapse one by one, first the door, then the ceiling, lifted like the roof of a dollhouse, and then the four walls fall outward. Night comes into the room, with its stars and invisible rivers. A single sentence was all it took to blow it down: *there is no frigate like a book.*

At school, Millicent learns arithmetic and geometry. But math is more than that, her father explains to her.

'Did you know numbers are infinite?' he asks her.

'They are infinite?'

'Yes, you can count forever. Take the largest number you can imagine, and you can still add 1.'

Millicent thinks for a few seconds, but David is already moving on.

'Do you know what is even more marvellous still?'

'No.'

'Numbers are just as infinite in either direction; you can count back in negative numbers without ever reaching the beginning.'

So that means you can also subtract forever; something always remains. The numbers grow as they are removed. Millicent feels like this is a bit of a sleight of hand, but she can't put her finger on what she finds unsettling, when David says, 'There is one more still.'

She looks up at him, wonders whether this is another trick, if this new infinity extends up and down, if it spirals or ascends diagonally.

'Between numbers,' David says, 'between one and two, you see, there are as many decimals as between zero and infinity.'

Millicent sighs with relief. At last, this third infinity, this smaller infinity, seems easier to inhabit.

Once a week, Lavinia still goes into Emily's bedroom to remove imaginary dust. Behind the white of the curtain, the sky is whiter still. And what is behind the sky? Armed with a feather duster and a rag, she carefully wipes the waxed surfaces of the chest of drawers, the wardrobe, and the small desk. This morning, for the first time – how could she not have seen it before? – she notices, on the edge of the desk, an area half the size of a fingernail where the varnish has been scuffed, exposing the pale, bare wood similar to skin. Lavinia puts her fingertip on this other fingertip in the wood and gently scratches, as if to awaken a little animal. Then she goes down to the cellar, where she stores the onions, potatoes, beets, and nuts. She feels around for a nut, goes back up to the kitchen and cracks the shell with the silver nutcracker. In her palm, the two hemispheres of the walnut grooved with deep bands make her think of a tiny brain.

She climbs the stairs back to the bedroom, kneels in front of the desk so she can see better, and rubs the nut on the wood. Miraculously, the space is filled in, the pale depression is permeated with a warm caramel colour that melts into the varnish covering the rest of the desk. She considers the result from different angles, leaning her head in every direction, gives it a final touch-up and then, satisfied, since nothing should ever be wasted, she bites into what remains of the nut before going back down to the kitchen where a small box of oranges awaits her.

Even in summer, the fruit is expensive and hard to find, but the zest of a single orange will aromatize up to eight jars of cranberry jelly. Once the zest is removed, the fruit doesn't keep for long. It is best to eat the flesh that day. Most people carefully separate the sections to sample them slowly one by one, making the pleasure last. Lavinia prefers to bite into the whole fruit, as you would bite into an apple, the juice running down her chin, her fingers, a bath of orange that will be her perfume for hours.

When she goes out in town, people want to hear the latest news, chat, and exchange gossip. She firmly turns the gossips away.

'I don't have time. I have places to go.'

She walks to the cemetery. She leaves two jars of cranberry jelly on Emily's grave, removing the lids to make a feast for the bees. In May, June, and July, her sister's grave is the downiest, most golden and honeyed in the cemetery.

Then she stops to reflect at Sophia's grave. In her peripheral vision, she spots three little ghosts who burst out laughing when they see her weighed down by the years, and they take off skipping through the graves. She has just encountered her childhood.

Something strikes her in that moment, in the bright sunlight: the ghosts don't live in her house, nor even in the cemetery. She is the one they haunt, and she carries them wherever she goes. She is, we are all, nesting Russian dolls, made of ghosts, memories, the departed, down to the heart of wood that is both living and dead, always at risk of going up in flames.

❧

When she misses her sister too much, Lavinia takes a flask, a dropper, two, three little drops of bitter liquid on a sugar cube, and knows she will see her in her dreams.

Emily is barely more diaphanous, more ethereal, than she was in life. She always had a flowing step, as if she were floating a few inches from the ground. Emily slips to the wardrobe and opens the doors. Inside hang seven flamboyant dresses, one for each day of the week: dandelion, pumpkin, poppy, raspberry, aubergine, pistachio, teal. She takes the teal one and throws it on. She is as pretty as a peacock.

'We will need to clean up the capital letters,' Higginson says to Mabel, as he reads her selection of poems.

'What do you mean "clean up"?'

'There are obviously too many.'

She has put fastidious care into first copying out the poems exactly as Emily had written them, dashes and capitals included, before making a second more legible version. There are almost no dashes left (she is a little annoyed with herself for not having taken Lavinia's side the day she had the chance to), but the capitals seem to her fairly important. Diplomatically, at first she agrees.

'Of course, I copied them all faithfully so we could discuss them and together decide on the rule to follow. I was waiting to get your thoughts on it.'

'You do well. The rule is as follows: in English, we use capital letters for proper nouns, for the pronoun I, or to start a sentence or a verse.

Mabel waits for the rest, which does not come. She takes a sheet at random among those on the table and reads aloud:

The last Night that She lived
It was a Common Night
Except the Dying – this to Us
Made Nature different

Showing Higginson the paper, she goes through the list.

'There are seven capital letters here, in addition to those that start the verse: *Night, She, Common, Night, Dying, Us, Nature*.

As she lists them, it seems to her that these seven words are a poem within a poem, like seeds inside the apple, potential fruit. Surely Higginson must also see that that is the heart of the little paper creature.

But instead he says, 'These extra capitals are like the dashes that we eliminated: they only hamper reading. The eye needs fluidity, Mrs. Todd.'

'Certainly, but' – and why does an image inspired by David come to mind? – 'don't you think that the seven words in a way form a little constellation among the stars of the poem that the reader has to connect above all the others that shine less bright?'

This time, Higginson laughs a little, kindly. 'You should have been a poet yourself, my dear madam.'

Mabel has to restrain herself from shouting at him to stop calling her *madam*. In a supremely controlled voice, she manages to suggest, 'Very well, but maybe in keeping some of these capital letters, half, let's say, we can preserve the accent Emily chose to place on some words? The word *Night*, for example, written twice with a capital letter, and then *She*, and surely also *Nature*?'

'Did Emily Dickinson ever write to you, Mrs. Todd?'

The question catches Mabel off guard.

'Yes, a few times. I still have her letters at home.'

'You do well to keep them. She wrote me dozens of letters over the years, hundreds of pages, and each one was strewn with capital letters as fanciful as they are useless. She had no concern for such things; she wrote haphazardly. Are you suggesting we also keep the spelling mistakes in these texts?'

That day, it is Mabel who feels the fierce need to save these *mistakes*, all the mistakes Emily made, unjustified, unforgivable, these crimes against grammar, the hundred ways she found to subvert the language to make each of these poems a tiny foreign land.

'Where is Miss Emily?' Millicent asks, looking at Homestead through the window after the editor has left.

Her mother and father exchange glances. He answers, in a gentle voice, 'She died last year, my darling. I'm not surprised you wouldn't remember; you never saw her.'

'I know very well she's dead, but I wanted to know where she is.'

'She is in heaven,' Mabel says.

'In heaven?'

'After death, good people spend eternity in paradise, and bad people are sent to hell forever.'

'And who decides?'

'Our Lord decides, in His infinite wisdom.'

Millicent reflects. She has never seen Our Lord either. Maybe, like Miss Emily, He doesn't like to leave His house.

'And am I good or bad?'

'You are good, my darling, of course. Like me, like your father.'

'Do the bad people know they are going to hell?'

'I don't really know, well, yes, they must.'

Mabel casts a desperate glance at David. Theology has never been her strong suit. She didn't think she would be required to wade in so far. She feels quickly out of her depth.

'Because if they know,' Millicent says, with the unyielding logic of a nine-year-old, 'either they have chosen to go, and then it is not a punishment, or they can't help being bad, in which case how can Our Lord punish them?'

Another urgent look. This time, David intervenes. 'Some people believe that after death there is neither heaven nor hell. We fall asleep and we never wake up, that's all. What do you think of that?'

Millicent tries to picture sleep – a dream – that would last for eternity. Her father goes on.

'Other people think we come back to Earth many times, that we have many lives.'

'Really?'

Mabel makes a slight click of her tongue to show that she does not appreciate the turn the conversation has taken, but her disapproval is not such that she feels the strength to take back control.

'And can you choose what you come back as?' Millicent asks.

'I don't know,' David says. 'But if you could, what would you choose? A cat? A whale?'

'Could I be your little girl again?'

'I hope so, yes.'

Millicent finally seems settled again.

'And Miss Emily, what do you think she would come back as?' Millicent asks.

'I don't know, my love. I didn't know her well enough. A gull, perhaps? They say she really liked white, and birds.'

The little girl thinks a moment longer, gesturing to the papers spread on the table.

'Maybe she doesn't need to come back. Maybe she is still here.'

Things that live in the sky

Birds
Dragonflies
Clouds
Bats
Stars
The moon
Miss Emily

On one of the first notes Emily sent Susan over thirty years earlier it reads, in a shaky pen: *Open me carefully.* In the little parlour plunged in darkness, Susan absentmindedly traces her finger over the paper, astonished that she can still feel the skin-like grain.

This night, from Emily's letters emerges a girl of fifteen, sixteen, twenty years old, solar, light, alive as water. The figure is not the figure of Emily, but of Susan, for whom the words of her friend written decades earlier restore life in her in that moment. Between these lines, Susan sees all the potential Susans, among whom she had not yet chosen; she finds all the ones she left behind, until she is no more than an empty husk. One by one, they stand, an army of women, from youth to maturity, start walking with the same step that has always been hers, and which she had forgotten when she fell in step with others. They will not lie back down.

Susan gets up last, goes to the window and parts the curtain to look outside. The sky is a navy blue, the sun has not yet appeared. No matter, she can wait. Dawn will come. She has her whole life ahead of her.

One day a seasonal worker comes to knock at the door of Homestead. He offers to prepare the fallow field for next year's sowing, to patch the roof of the barn, to do any odd jobs Lavinia cares to assign him. In exchange, he asks for next to nothing: a place to sleep, two meals a day, one dollar a week. He wears a wide-brimmed hat that hides half his eyes, but his smile is forthright, and one shouldn't leave land fallow for too long.

Holden – his name – sleeps in the barn with his dog, an animal with long red fur. There are often bits of straw in his hair, which is as blond as wheat.

Lavinia sees him only at noon, when she goes to give him both his lunch and his dinner, wrapped in pristine table-cloths. Simple meals that don't easily spoil in the heat: sand-wiches, marinated vegetables, slices of ham and hard-boiled eggs on nests of ice, and every day one apple to crunch for noon and another for the evening. As if for a horse, she can't help but think.

❧

In the afternoon, she stretches out on her sister's bed, toes pointed to the ceiling; she crosses her hands over her chest and closes her eyes. The house is quiet. She holds her breath. Thirty seconds. One minute. Pepper, who has followed her, comes to cautiously sniff at this body that has stopped breathing. Without opening her eyes, Lavinia turns her head to the window and her eyelids are papered with vermilion, turning to carnation, then to a brilliant coral, the brightest colour she has ever seen, eyes open or closed. She doesn't know whether the blaze comes from the fire of the sun or her heart, which is threatening to burst.

It is apricot season: small, firm, velvety fruit, with their fragrant flesh that smells of honey and white flowers. Lavinia delicately slices them, setting aside the sections, which she sprinkles with a bit of sugar, and then she places the pits on her work surface. Using a little wooden mallet, she breaks the hard shells to reveal the kernel, the secret heart that less seasoned cooks throw away, even though inside it lies the source of the vanilla aroma of the fruit. She boils the kernels for one minute, takes them out of the water to peel them down to their white flesh. The exposed stones have a consistency similar to chestnuts, and she will grind them to add them to the filing for her pie – apricots, honey, vanilla, and a few tablespoons of rum. This is what has earned her first place in the pastry competition at the town fair four years running.

She takes from the icebox the pastry she had placed in there to chill, rolls it out, working it as little as possible so as not to melt the butter, transfers it to the dish, and slips it in the oven to blind bake after pouring into it a shower of dried peas, which have turned a golden brown hue through more than ten years of being used for this very purpose. Once the crust is precooked, she pours in the filling in a stream of golden orange. She saves enough pastry for a simple braid over the fruit, then she brushes it with a mixture of egg and milk and puts it back in the oven.

When she takes the apricot pie from the oven three quarters of an hour later, she realizes that she will not be able to swallow so much as a bite. For a moment, she considers bringing it to Evergreens, but Susan hardly eats anymore, and Austin is never there.

Lavinia cuts a slice of her useless pie, places it on a plate and heads to the barn. A ray of light slips under the door that she cracks open in silence. He is sitting there, not far from Hector the horse, his back resting against the wall, his legs stretched in front of him, his dog curled up at his side. He is reading a book she recognizes, and to see him engrossed in *Leaves of Grass* fills her with inexplicable emotion. She makes two sharp knocks on the open panel, places the slice of pie on the ground, and turns on her heels before he has time to rise.

'Wait!' she hears him behind her, but Lavinia doesn't turn. And then, 'Thank you!'

The light that flows over the field when she heads back to the house is just as golden, just as thick as her apricot caramel; the sun, a ripe piece of fruit.

To keep an exact count of the days, Mabel maintains two logs of her existence, each scrupulously precise: a journal and a diary. In the first, she records the weather, the day's activities, visits received or rendered, books read, exhibitions seen, trips taken; in the second, she notes her thoughts and emotions, details her grievances, her hopes, plumbs the movements of her heart and her soul. That is where she enters, excitedly, an *fm* or a trembling # each time she has intimate relations with David or Austin, with a dash on the days when she achieves ecstasy, that glimpse of paradise after dinner, as she likes to say to one or the other. This paradise now exists twofold: having been reached in the arms of her husband or her lover, then having been set on paper by a sort of invisible witness Mabel takes with her everywhere, the audience without whom she stops believing in the spectacle of her life.

While naturally given to more lofty considerations, she cannot drive out a frugal core that makes her count and recount these signs like the miser counts with sensual pleasure the gold coins that make up his fortune. Sometimes, she gives in to the thought that these written traces are more precious to her than the embraces they represent; the embraces last only a moment, these exist forever. Turning the pages of her diary, she contemplates this succession of petites morts with profound satisfaction. Of all her collections, this is the one that gives her the most joy.

࢙

In the middle of the night, she wakes up drenched, throws off the duvet. Beside her, David is faintly snoring and turns over, pulling on the sheet. It is the same panic that drags her from sleep several times a week, an unfocused emergency, a clock beating in her chest asking her what she will have done with her days by the end of her life. Other women have children until they drown out this tick-tock, but Millicent more than suffices; there are even moments – God forgive her – when she tries to picture her existence if she hadn't had her daughter. Would she have dared run away with Austin, making a whole new life with him, far from everything? But that is not what plagues her. What wakes her up at night is not yet having completed a work worthy of the name, nothing that may survive her, nothing she will be remembered for after her death. Emily's poems have eternity before them, but Mabel is cruelly aware that the same is not true for her.

She discovered a few days earlier that she was born the year Austin and Susan were married. To think of this again gives her the horrible feeling that she could be their daughter. She tosses and turns in the bed that is too soft, ends up getting up to go to the window. It is a dark night outside; she can barely make out the silhouette of Evergreens where Austin is sleeping next to his wife. Mabel shivers, and a warm hand is placed on her shoulder. She hadn't heard David get up. He presses his body against hers through the thin fabric of the nightgown, she turns, they embrace, then David takes her in his arms, brings her back to bed, places his hands on her hips. For a few minutes, she forgets all the books she hasn't written.

When she gets up the next morning, she has a headache. She has a sharp pain in her lower belly, and she fears, after ten years of peace, that she is pregnant again despite taking precautions. In that moment, she would like to be a hay.

'And what's this one?'
'Nettle.'
'What is it for?'
'It is excellent for rheumatism.'
'Oh.'

The two women are standing in front of the glass-paned kitchen cupboard where Lavinia keeps, in identical glass jars, mixtures of dried flowers and leaves, which some ladies in town claim are more effective than the pharmacopoeia prescribed by the apothecary. She is particularly proud of this collection amassed over the years, and she gladly shares its benefits with those who ask.

'And this one?' Mabel asks, indicating another jar filled with dried leaves and yellow-grey flower buds.

'It is a mixture of lemon balm and chamomile.'
'And what is it used for?'
'When taken as an infusion before bed, it helps you sleep.'
'I see.'

Mabel continues to review the jars where teas and dried herbs slumber, as if she were looking for a title in an unfamiliar library.

'This one?'

Lavinia starts to get impatient. 'Licorice and anise. Are you suffering from cramps?'

'No.'

'Then you don't need it.'

'And this one …'

This time, Lavinia doesn't let her finish her question. 'It would be simpler if you would tell me exactly what you want.'

Mabel, known for her boldness and self-confidence, suddenly feels her cheeks flush. Without daring to look at the woman she sees as her sister-in-law, while being cruelly aware that this is not reciprocated, she whispers, 'I am looking for something that would prevent … Something that would guarantee … I love my daughter, you know. Of course I love her. But I don't want … Well, it would be regrettable that …'

'You don't want another child.'

'That's it. If you know of a way, please, tell me.'

She doesn't dare evoke the figure of Austin, but both feel his shadow hover over the kitchen.

'Yes, it just so happens I know a way,' Lavinia says.

Mabel waits, hanging on her words.

'It's simple: you stop having relations.'

It is not hard to distinguish on the table piles of poems sorted and transcribed from the little heap of sheets that remain to be inventoried. Millicent makes her selection from the latter, one scrap of paper at a time, purposely not looking at what is written on them, to make the surprise last. Sometimes, despite herself, a few words leap out at her – *perhaps, heaven, daffodil* – but more often, closing her eyes, she starts by bringing the paper to her nose to breathe it in with the same delight that she breathes in her mother's bottles of perfume, carved in crystal.

Today's poem smells of cinnamon. She sets it carefully among the previous ones, which are scented with flower, brown sugar, and nutmeg. Mabel has never had the soul of a baker, so this is the first time Millicent has made a cake.

Then she points her kaleidoscope at a scrap of paper on which Emily has written her verse. A white star appears, six regular points, a snowflake. She turns slowly to the tipping point, and very fine lines emerge, made up half of letters, a quarter of sighs, dashes upside down, which together form a new alphabet. The poem is written in an invented language that never stops changing under her fingers, a language that is always new, forever foreign.

᪒

Some days, in the forest, she ignores the giant hardwoods whose arms hold up the sky and lies down on the ground to watch worms, beetles, and ants, which are her favourite. When she spots an anthill, she plants herself in front of it and watches the movement of the workers who leave and return in a long, black ribbon that gleams in the sun. Some bring back pieces of leaf bigger than themselves, others bring moults of insects, crumbs, or bits of mushrooms. The ants disappear underground one by one through an entrance; others come out through a neighbouring hole, and Millicent wonders whether they are the same ones, an unbroken loop, or whether they are new ones each time – but then how many insects can an anthill hold? Is it infinite? Do they create new ones every second? Are they all different like snowflakes in a cloud?

A bird perches on a low branch and watches Millicent. It looks like a pigeon that has been cut out of white paper. She approaches quietly, so as not scare it off, but the bird isn't afraid. It stares at her without blinking. Millicent watches its down rustling in the breeze, like very fine snow. The bird has a coral beak and feet, black, brilliant eyes encircled with a thin ring in the same pink as her own eyelid. Its plumage is immaculate.

The two creatures remain connected through their eyes until the bird spreads its wings and takes flight. One part of Millicent, the secret, silent part, disappears with him. This part knows how to fly.

During the hours spent immobile, she has mastered the art of spotting the tiniest details: a rustling of the leaves that reveals the presence of a chipmunk, an owl sleeping camouflaged in a hole in an oak, a golden bud that shimmers in the high grass, a chartreuse caterpillar hanging from a swinging thread like a pendulum between sky and earth.

Once she goes back inside, she can't help herself; Millicent continues to see what others miss: the bills piling up in the kitchen, a little hole in the wallpaper in the dining room, the pink that rushes to her mother's cheeks where Mr. Dickinson is concerned.

❧

One morning, Millicent decides she too will make a book with flowers.

In the forest, she chooses them carefully. Likewise in the garden, in Mrs. Hansel's flower beds, slipping in when her neighbour is out. Her satchel is stuffed when she heads home to spread the flowers between the pages of her encyclopedia. Patiently, she counts the days and weeks before returning to pick them again, once dried, like cut-out drawings. Then she glues them in families and in bouquets, as she has seen in the herbariums she has consulted. But where yellow, purple, and pink creatures are usually displayed, on the pages Millicent has assembled only the white blooms of cosmos, daisies, nemesias. They are the only ones sufficiently like snowflakes.

A few months ago, we bought a piece of land the size of a small forest, on the side of a mountain in the Eastern Townships. For the moment, there is nothing on it: a few burnt-out cars from the 1950s or 1960s, fieldstone walls built by hand, covered over the years with moss, likely meant to contain the water from a few streams (we counted four) that wind through the property. Until the beginning of the 1940s, this land was cultivated; farm buildings burnt down one night were never rebuilt, and since then the land has been essentially abandoned. In the middle of the forest that has reasserted its rights, there is an orchard of a dozen apple trees with twisted branches, returned to their wild state. Elsewhere, there is the stone foundation of a construction that may have been a house.

From a plateau – the one with the orchard – through a gap in the trees, you can see the blue expanse of Brome Lake, then the mountains outlined in the distance. From here, there is no house in sight, not the slightest village, no road, no electrical wires. From here, it is 1890.

It was long believed that the word *forest* had a distant Germanic root, and that it derived from *forist*, which means 'pine'; then there was an attempt to relate it to the Roman *forum*, but it seems that the word comes instead from the Latin *foris*, which means 'outdoors.' In fairy tales, the forest is the place where one goes to lose children, a place with every possible danger in which, driven by curiosity, they get lost themselves. The forest is the opposite of home.

My father's family name, which I was given at birth, is a distortion of *Forestier*, or *Forester*, in English. *Forestis* is that which is found, literally, outside the enclosure. This is why in Italian the word *forestiero* today still means a stranger, a man who has come from outside or who lives outside, in any event a sort of savage. But this term *savage* comes in turn from another form of forest, *sylva* (which gave rise notably to *sylviculture*), from which *salvatacus* is later derived. The savage is the one who lives in the forest; the forester is the one who lives in savagery.

Among the trees, some dream of becoming ship, clog, cradle, house, swing, marionette, flute, piano. We make everything with trees – even books. Libraries are still forests. To open a book is to find oneself *outside* (of oneself, of the world around us) at the same time as one is closest to beings and one's own secrets through the miracle of this other world invented or plucked from time.

Of course, a tree that falls alone in the forest falls in silence. But what happens when someone falls in the forest without anyone hearing? Are they hurt? Will they get back up? Are they dead?

What remains is the real question, the one no one ever asks, which is: what about forests that are felled in their entirety, silently, within us? What happens when great swaths of our lives crumble, disappear, vanish, when on the surface nothing shows – not a scream or a ripple? Do they hollow out a void so deep it swallows us up, as black holes swallow everything that has the misfortune of passing within their reach, feeding their nothingness with the fire of stars?

Things that do not die

~~Oceans~~
~~Countries~~
~~Fire~~
~~Forests~~
~~Stars~~
Books

One morning, when Susan wakes up, rather than pulling her down toward the ground, her dead slowly get up with her. She takes them for a walk.

She goes to knock on Lavinia's door; Lavinia opens it, looking astonished, and shifts foot to foot, wondering whether she has to invite her in, as she would a visitor who was expected.

But Susan gets straight to the point. 'I've changed my mind.'

'Oh?'

Lavinia wipes her hands on her apron. What has her sister-in-law changed her mind about? Has she got it into her head to divorce Austin?

'Give me back the poems; I'm going to put together Emily's book.'

'Oh.'

She twists the apron in her fingers.

'Well,' Lavinia begins, 'I have entrusted them to someone highly qualified, and who knew our Emily very well, that dear Mr. Higginson, you know; he is very prominent, and he was very enthusiastic about the idea of having them printed.'

She stops, realizing that with all the *verys* she is only diluting what she is trying to convince Susan of. And yet it is not entirely false: Higginson is indeed working on the poems; it's just that it is not in his hands that she placed them.

Susan seems to realize that her sister-in-law is hiding something. She searches for the truth in Lavinia's eyes as she lowers her eyelids.

'Would you like a cup of tea?' Lavinia asks.

'No.'

Susan is not someone who believes that tea fixes everything. If only someone would offer her a cup of opium, a cup of hemlock, a cup of cocaine.

She turns on her heels.

'Dear Susan, we will save the first copy for you!' cries Lavinia, to her sister-in-law's hunched back as she leaves.

Lavinia spends the afternoon at the Todds', not because she particularly wants Mabel's company, but she wants to have tea with her sister and knows no other way. She picks up a poem, then another. Emily speaks to her of the paradise that is not at all how she imagined; it is a small ruby-coloured town, with roofs of feather and inhabitants as diaphanous as moths that bear the names of ducks. For a moment, Lavinia also lives in this little town; she too is a feathered thing.

Mabel takes the opportunity to show her the progress on the work; Lavinia leans over the table where the handwritten poems and their transcriptions sit side by side.

'What is this?' she asks, indicating, on a scrap of paper, three long horizontal dashes struck through with diagonal lines.

'These are the excess dashes Mr. Higginson talked about. Those are the ones I am suggesting deleting.'

Lavinia guardedly nods her head. In some books she has read, dashes are used in dialogue to indicate a change of speaker. If her sister's poems are dotted with them, could it be that she was expecting an answer?

She doesn't dare tell Mabel that under the long dashes she can hear her dead sister breathing.

᠉

It is almost dinnertime when Lavinia realizes she forgot to ask Holden to fix a broken rein. The light falls diagonally over the fields; on the path that leads to the barn, her shadow walks before her. She arrives while he is washing himself outdoors; the water streams down his back smooth as silk. His suspenders dangle on either side of his torso. His hair is wet, his arms lifted like a statue. Lavinia leaves without daring to bother him.

But how is it that, the next day at lunchtime, she again forgot to tell him about the broken rein? She has no choice but to walk the path to the barn again at the end of the day. He is outdoors like the day before, water runs down his back, and she feels like the day is repeating itself, or that she dreamed the first one. But what happens next has never happened before: she approaches, bends over, takes the sponge near the bucket of soapy water and gently passes it over Holden's shoulders, as she would for a child or an animal she were afraid of startling. He turns slowly. He is not surprised to see her there.

Lavinia is the one who leads the way to the barn. She is the one who unbuttons his pants and helps him remove the layers that cover her like onion skin: skirt, underskirt, stockings, chemise, corset, underwear. His rough hands, calloused and cracked, snag on the simple lace that adorns her women's clothing, like thistles on the coats of cats. But his gestures are confident and gentle.

Afterward, as they are lying under the wool blanket that covers his straw mattress, she asks him, 'So how old are you?'

'Thirty-four.'

He doesn't ask her the question in return. She would lie to him. Or she would tell the truth: that in this very moment, she too is thirty-four.

❧

She goes to join him before sunrise, slips into the barn at first light, lies down next to him, and awakens him by kissing his neck. He recognizes her in his sleep, reaches out his arm in a dream, pulls her to him. Together they watch the coming of the day through the gaps in the boards; every morning is the first time and the last. Lavinia is never sure she will come back the next day; before going to him, she is not even sure she went the day before.

These silent encounters occur outside time, in another life that does not belong to either of them and that they can inhabit only together, as if each has half the key to open the lock. Lavinia starts to dream that she leaves the big house with its sleeping ghosts to come rest here, on the golden straw, with Holden and the dog who runs in its dreams.

The days go by, and she does not ask him other questions. She knows his name, and that he has soft lips: what more does she need to know? But her lack of curiosity surprises him.

'You never ask me anything, Lavinia,' he points out one evening. 'Not where I come from, or how much longer I plan to stay, not where I'll go next, whether I have any brothers or sisters …'

'That's true.'

Silence. He waits, then, as she says nothing, he goes on. 'Don't people who want to get to know each other normally ask those sorts of questions?'

'I don't know what people normally do. What do you want me to ask you?' she says. Under her hand, she feels him shrug. She interrupts his gesture, sighs, and speaks. 'Very well, where are you from?'

'Springfield, Ohio.'

More silence. What does one say to someone from Springfield, Ohio? But he asks her in turn, 'And where are you from?'

With her hand, she gestures to the big vanilla house and the town beyond.

'You were born in Amherst?'

'I was born in this house. I have lived almost nowhere else.'

'Isn't it big to live in all by yourself?'

He asked the question innocently. He is not angling for an invitation; Lavinia is sure of that. She is nonetheless cut to the quick.

'I'm not alone,' she replies, a little more curtly than intended.

She holds back from adding, 'I have my cats,' which could send her into the territory of pitiful comedy, the last place in the world she wants to be. They stand up, collect their clothes, and each gets dressed in their own corner.

'Oh, I thought … ' Holden begins, but doesn't know how to finish the sentence.

Of course, he would have heard about Emily's death.

'Yes, well,' Lavinia answers. 'You will forgive me if I don't ask you how long you plan to stay, or whether you have any brothers or sisters.'

She is upset with herself for having said this. What is she trying to punish him for?

She leaves without looking back into the falling night and the song of the last cicadas, piercing and metallic, which leaves the taste of iron in her mouth. Of course she is not all alone in the big house; as soon as she pushes open the door, her ghosts are there to greet her: Father, Mother, Emily. It is and will always be their home; she sees them sitting in the dining room, coming down the stairs. She watches them live and die again many times a day.

All night, she tosses and turns in her bed, throwing off the covers as if to drive away arms trying to enfold her. The next day, making her breakfast, she repeats several times, to practise saying it without her voice trembling, 'I think it's time for you to go.'

That is what she announces to Holden as she sets the tray in front of the barn door. Then, immediately, as if she already regrets her words, 'Of course, you can stay a few days, until you work out where to go. Until the end of the week, if you like.'

By evening, he is gone, but not far. The next week, unexpectedly spotting his silhouette in Georgina Wilson's field, Lavinia feels a pang in her heart and has to stop. Under the three o'clock sun, he reminds her of a painting by a French artist, a beautiful, light-filled piece that she saw only once, the main subject of which did not seem to be the man standing in the wheat field but the golden light he was bathed in, or, rather, the friendship between the light and the man. But she has never understood anything about painting. Emily could have at least told her the name of the artist, and no doubt that Lavinia had it all wrong, that the subject of the painting was in fact the sky that lay above the characters, or the shadow stretched out at their feet.

Holden doesn't see her standing on the road and keeps working. His movements are slow, powerful, and regular. Lavinia feels something like a sob rise in her throat, and she quickly starts walking again.

At the general store, she learns that he is now boarding in the room Georgina normally rents for a few dollars a week, and that the landlady is spoiling her new hired hand, bringing up a hot breakfast on a tray at dawn, as if he were staying at a hotel. Lavinia nods her head in silence, pays for her flour, and leaves. She takes a long detour to avoid walking past the field on the way home, but it is no use. She continues to see him; his image has been burned into her retina, or even deeper.

Millicent places on her desk the poem she pilfered the night before: five lines, eight words crossed out. She recopies the first word once, twice, three times, without tiring, until she has written it exactly as Miss Emily had done, striving to reproduce not only the line, the impression left on the page, but the gesture responsible for it, discernable in how the characters get thinner and thicker depending on whether the hand pressed more or less on the pen, the slight trembling in a few letters, the ink that accumulated where Emily interrupted her movement to think or watch the flight of a bee. Beyond the gesture, she feels like she has found the impetus that created it. She moves on to the second word, then the third. An hour goes by, and she is only halfway through the second line. She doesn't care. The line and a half are perfect. It is her greatest work to date; she may never do anything this good again in her life.

She makes a point not to dip her pen in the inkwell more often than Miss Emily did, a way of holding her breath as long as her, lacking the ability to synchronize the beating of their hearts. Soon, she will challenge herself to invent new sequences, starting with simple words, but ones that Emily never used: *zebra* (which she particularly likes because it starts with *z*), *canopea*, *Peru*. Then, naturally, she starts weaving her words together like the flower stems she uses to makes crowns.

All of this, the girl, who is left-handed, draws with her right hand to be certain to never, out of laziness or distraction, use her usual calligraphy to overcome or bypass a difficulty. At age ten, she is learning how to write again for the first time.

In her bedroom, Millicent religiously practises the violin a half hour a day, as she has been told to do, her fingers giving birth to nasal sounds like the squeak of a pulley. When she reached the age when little girls must apply themselves to learning music, Mabel, for appearances, had given her the choice.

'What instrument would you like to play, darling?'

The piano has always had a place of honour in the parlour. Mabel sits at it at least one hour per day to limber up her fingers and gladly performs whenever there is a visitor to the house, in addition to playing when she is asked – which is to say without fail – at soirees to which she is invited. This is part of the long list of things that make her marvellous.

As she answered, Millicent felt like the piano was looking at both of them with its dozens of ivory eyes. She had taken a deep breath and said, 'I would like to play the violin, please.'

'What?'

At first Mabel thought it was a joke, but Millicent never joked.

'I would like to play the violin,' her daughter repeated.

'But … but, I don't know how to play the violin!' Mabel exclaimed. 'I won't be able to teach you!'

Millicent had innocently looked down at her ankle boots – beige, a little scuffed at the toes, with sixteen eyelets (eight on the left, eight on the right) on each foot.

'That sounds like an excellent idea,' interjected David, who ordered the little violin the next day.

When the instrument arrived, it was a pretty amber colour. It was made of such smooth wood that it might have been the softest thing Millicent had ever touched in her life. Her teacher, a local young man named George, who had the beginnings of a goatee and no moustache at all, came once a week to give her lessons.

When Mabel opened the door to him, he seemed to forget why he was there, discussing with her the latest recitals that had been given in town, operas that were being staged in Boston and New York, his mad dream of becoming a soloist. She listened to him, head slightly tilted, eyes shining, a smile on her lips, as if this entirely unremarkable adolescent were the most fascinating person she had ever met. Eventually and regretfully he would break away from the mother to go upstairs to explain to the mousy little girl in a white dress where to put her little finger on the E-string to play a clear *sol*.

If she were asked to name her favourite things in the world, Millicent would say: books, fish, the moon, her father, perhaps in that order. And she would immediately have reproached herself for not having included Mabel.

Lavinia stops at the barn at the end of the afternoon, opens the door, enters cautiously, and breathes in the fragrance of cut hay. She turns around as if to ensure no one is following her, that she won't be seen. There is a sudden flash in the straw bed. Bending down, she discovers, between golden twigs, a silver medallion with the profile of the Virgin. A needle in a haystack. She turns it over in her hand; it is a cheap piece of jewellery, unrefined, probably produced by the hundreds, even thousands. She squeezes it so hard in the palm of her hand that the shape is imprinted in her flesh: a pink oval in the middle of the palm, like a scar.

She first considers slipping it in an envelope and bringing it to the post office, but despite herself her feet take her to Georgina Wilson's, who greets her with some astonishment.

'Lavinia! What a lovely surprise! You don't drop by often enough. Are you here about the fair?'

'No, I am here to see Holden. I have something of his, and I would like to return it.'

'I will get him right away.'

'Don't go to any trouble. I'll go up.'

'I'm not sure that is appropriate,' Georgina replies, with a little laugh to convey that they are both long past the age where anyone would be concerned about their virtue.

Lavinia climbs the stairs, wondering at each step what she is doing there, but the voice asking the question fades a little with each step. She knocks softly at the door; he opens it and looks at her in silence. He is taller than she remembered, more tanned, blonder too.

'I found a medallion in the hay,' says Lavinia.

He reaches out his open hand, and she places the face of the Madonna in it. He thanks her with a nod and is gently closing the door when she hears herself saying, 'Would you like to come for tea?'

さ

She has placed a bouquet of violets in the middle of the small round kitchen table, put on a new lace collar, smoothed her hair with particular care, with the tip of her index put two drops of vanilla in the hollow of her neck. It is the first time she has invited a boy to her house; she is as intimidated as if he were going to have to brave Father and Mother, endure Austin's taunts, suffer Emily's implacable examination. She does everything backwards; if she keeps it up, she will become little eight-year-old Lavinia again with her crooked braids and missing front tooth.

Holden has also brought violets, which she somehow adds to the little vase where she has already placed hers; it is complete disarray, lush and purple. They sit down awkwardly; she measures out the tea leaves, pours the hot water, offers milk and sugar, and they drink in polite sips. At least the lemon cake is perfect.

Lavinia clears her throat before asking, 'Tell me, where are you from? How long do you intend to stay in Amherst? Do you have any brothers or sisters?'

And then, 'Is Holden your first or last name?'

Though they are neighbours, Austin and Mabel write to each other ten, twenty times a week, letters that form between the two houses an eternal paper bridge, which Susan, who says nothing about it, dreams of setting on fire. For Mabel, these letters are as necessary as air and water. Without them, she would forget to believe in Austin's love as soon as he is out of sight. These papers are ten, one hundred, one thousand times her lover under her touch.

Sitting at her dressing table after breakfast, she hastily writes out the words she will whisper to him when they are reunited in the evening: *My darling beloved – & my king & master – my gentle husband*, for the pleasure of seeing the shadow of his hand write her in return: *My darling beloved, my queen and mistress, my gentle wife …*

She needs these two loves, the domestic and the adulterous. Complementary, necessary to each other, they give her the exhilarating impression of living as she watches herself live – even better, to no longer be confined to a single life. She would not admit it to either David or Austin, but she sometimes even finds herself regretting that her lover cannot see how beautiful she is in the arms of her husband.

David looks up at the sky. With his eyes closed, he could name the stars that form familiar figures, the big and little dippers, the hunter and his dog. That evening, the brightest light does not come from Venus, but from the window of the red house where he saw Mabel enter, followed by Mr. Dickinson a few moments later. The class he was to teach at the college was cancelled at the last minute; he took his time going home and even so arrived too early. He stands in front of his house like a guest who has been shown the door.

He is in no way unaware of Austin's visits to Mabel, of the presents he gives his wife, of the letters they exchange almost daily, even though they manage to see each other almost every day. This in no way pleases him. Of course, he would have chosen otherwise. But it makes Mabel so happy, and she is so pretty when she smiles that he doesn't have the heart to reproach her.

ॐ

Every evening, by candlelight, David creates for his daughter a theatre of shadow puppets in which birds morph into elephants, which in turn transform into palm trees, before hopping away once they have become rabbits. She looks at the wall, fascinated by the magic playing out on it that her father knows how to create out of next to nothing: light and his ten fingers.

One day, after tucking her in, he presents her with a riddle.

'You can see me with your eyes and smell me with your nose, but you can't touch me. I alone in this world do not have a shadow. Who am I?'

She thinks long and hard and guesses, 'Another shadow?'

He laughs. 'Good try. But can you smell a shadow with your nose?'

Crestfallen, she allows that you can't. She tries again. 'The hand of a clock?'

'No.'

More silence. Another try. 'The ocean?'

'No, but you are not as far off as you think; it is the opposite. Think about it until tomorrow night. If you haven't found the answer by then, I will show you.'

She falls asleep right away, has dreams filled with elephants light as feathers, flights of doves, all the shadow creatures that are the companions of her nights. She spends the next day searching for her own shadow, as if to sneak up on it, force it to reveal its secret. In vain. The shadow remains silently stretched out at her feet, except at noon, when it disappears.

The next evening, when her father presents her with the riddle again, Millicent gives up. David takes a box of matches out of his pocket, strikes one, but, rather than immediately igniting the candle he is using as a source of light, he says to his daughter, 'Look at the wall.'

She turns. In the light of the moon, the shadow of the candle can be made out on the wall, clearly; you can even see the very slightly curved tip of the wick.

'Is it lit or out?' David asks.

'Out.'

'Turn around.'

The wick is flaming, yellow, orange, almost alive.

Millicent turns again to the wall, where no flame dances.

'Fire,' she whispers. 'Fire has no shadow.'

Enchanted, she stares at this little flame that is light twice over: in the glow it produces, in the darkness it does not.

That evening, as she falls asleep, she finds another answer to her father's question: Miss Emily's poems do not have a shadow. Her poems *are* pale shadows, texts woven from the silence between words, a house made of windows.

Sitting at a celestial table, Emily, Sophia, and Gilbert are busy folding and cutting white paper. They do so with great care, taking one sheet at a time, folding it in two, in four, then in eight, before using scissors to cut out the first piece, each time sculpting a different motif: star, flower, thorn, which are repeated six times identically when the sheet is unfolded. Their work complete, they let them go, and the little paper creatures drift away, carried on the wind.

Lifting her eyes to look out the window, Millicent sees a flake fall, then a second, tiny and unhurried. She read in an issue of *National Geographic* that the Scots have hundreds of words for snow. A large flake is a *skelf*, fine snow that is starting to fall is called *sneesl*, whirlwinds are called *feefle*, powder is called *snaw-pouther*, while *flindrikin* means gentle snow. To name what is falling today from the sky in a very light, whirling powder, one would have to search even further; each storm is unique, like each of the flakes that make it up – for each one we would need an all-white hapax. Millicent dreams for a moment of being able to capture all of them to make a herbarium with as many pages as there are hours in a life, a true snow book.

Snow isn't white, she sees that now. No more than is the fire of stars, which are simply too far away for us to make out their colours. Perhaps snow is too close? Things are never where we expect them to be, or maybe she is not where she should be. When evening comes and the shadows grow longer, snow is blue like the sky. In the morning, it is the pink light of clouds at dawn, the thousand shimmers of the nacre of a single oyster.

She doesn't know what to do with this new knowledge: the world is an oyster.

The next evening, while her mother is working by lamplight, impatient, irritated at not getting anything done, Millicent approaches the table. Mabel doesn't send her off right away, too busy trying to decipher four verses that she can't shed any light on. She sighs, exasperated, calls David for help, shows him the scrap of paper on which he can't make out the obscure characters either. He attempts an interpretation, she suggests another, and they debate. Millicent hardly needs to come closer; the letters jump out at her. The hours spent in the company of ants have taught her the chicken scratch. She reads the text out loud without hesitation, as easily as if it were printed in tidy characters.

> *I cannot live with you,*
> *It would be life,*
> *And life is over there*
> *Behind the shelf.*

What she has read is midway between what David suspected and Mabel proposed. Both were half right, wrong in equal measure. Without her, they never would have got it.

'Say that again,' says Mabel, incredulous.

Millicent does as she is told. In the same even voice, she recites the verse they were struggling so hard to decipher. Emily's words, scribbled, crossed out, half erased, struck through, littered with silences and invented punctuation, are to her a sort of second mother tongue, both clear and mysterious, as natural as that of the birds and the tall oaks. She strings them together as one would play a score, as one would walk without sinking into the snow on an already broken trail, knowing precisely where to find her delicate balance.

With his magnifying glass, David leans over the text, repeats in a low voice his daughter's words. Millicent is right, that is perfectly obvious; she has solved the puzzle of the scribbles down to the most incomprehensible. Astonished, he asks her, 'How did you do that?'

She shrugs. 'You just have to know how to look.'

Back in her room, Millicent pulls scissors from her desk, takes a sheet that she folds two, three, four times, and that she notches to cut out triangles, half hearts, quarter stars, shapes that don't have a name and that are revealed only when the paper is unfolded. She takes a new sheet, makes a second snowflake, unique like the first. Then with a sort of quiet vengeance, she tears a sheet from her solfege workbook, which she cuts for the pleasure of inserting rests between the notes. Then she ends up taking, from under her mattress where she has hidden them, one of the stolen poems, the scraps of which rain down onto her feet to form other ephemeral, minuscule poems. It has become a kaleidoscope.

In her books of lists, she then notes, over many pages, conversations she will never have except in a dream, too timid to speak up before the rare beings she esteems or admires. And then, on the still blank page topped with the title *My best*

friends, in her round, determined handwriting, she enters: *Miss Emily*.

Seeing the swirling snowflakes through the window, the first of the year, Susan goes down, opens the door and, in just a taffeta dress, heads out into the garden already blanketed in white. The sun has recently set, the world is bathed in blue shadow. The wind blows through the branches, the snow whips her cheeks, slips down her neck, sticks to her hair, her face, but she doesn't care; she lifts her head to the sky, and, like when she was young, a young wife, a young mother, a young friend, she spreads her arms to embrace the storm or be carried away by it. Her wet clothes stick to her body; she should be shivering, but she doesn't feel the cold. She remains there, alone in the storm, a sort of long awakening.

Edward spots her through the window and calls to his sister. Both run out, grab her, and try to lead her back into the house, but Susan holds them back and pulls them to her. She has difficulty breathing, but it is not pain that is crushing her ribs; it is a sudden and almost agonizing gratitude to still have, in the middle of the storm, these two living children.

For a long time, I wished I had lived in the nineteenth century, which I saw as the backdrop of an existence without the thousand and one needless obligations that weigh down our modern, overstimulated lives. I felt like I was turning at breakneck speed on an unhinged carousel, wanting to slow its flight. This is why, I think, from the beginning, I was seeking in a hundred ways to stop time through my books: washing up for two years on the ice in the company of shipwrecked sailors; doing the same walk one hundred times and trying to write it in one hundred different ways; looking at the United States from so far away that it seemed like a multicoloured quilt; in stopping twenty, thirty minutes a day to think about what lettuce, potato, and colchicum inspire in me; trying to grasp the one thousand years that had swept over Mont-Saint-Michel; finding a moment every day to preserve like an insect in amber; dreaming, finally, of the life of a poet shut away in her bedroom who could imagine a whole field from just one clover, just one bee.

In March 2020, my wish was granted, and everyone was shut away at home, not allowed to leave except to buy food or medication. Everything else (stores, restaurants, gyms, even offices, factories, and schools) was closed. All that was left to do was to read, bake bread, knit, and make rounds of the neighbourhood on solitary walks, watch the light change while observing the almost motionless course of violet shadows over the snow, as one would watch the moon cross the sky, one millimetre of immensity at a time. For a few weeks, we all lived like Emily Dickinson.

❧

At that moment, on either side of the ocean, my French publisher and I were putting the final touches on the Grasset edition of *Les villes de papier*. We had never met; even after making this book together, we have never seen each other. She was locked down in a little apartment in Paris; I didn't dare say that in Outremont, I could leave my home every morning and climb Mont Royal with Sirius the dog, contemplate the deserted city at my feet, the sky stripped of its planes. That morning, after a long climb over the icy snow, at the top, the sun was white. There was not a sound, but you could hear the distant murmur of the city below. It was an inhabited silence, what the dead must hear when, tired of heaven, they turn their ear toward Earth.

On the mountain, the blue-white snow sparkled with a thousand tiny flashes, diamond dust. When Jacques Cartier's men thought they had discovered gold and precious stones on the rock of Cap Diamant, it was neither quartz nor iron pyrite they had seen, but no doubt snow, each flake shining like a star fallen from the sky.

In those days I felt, in the middle of the frozen city as I looked down on the roofs, steeples, smoking chimneys, a sense of freedom and solitude so great that sometimes I had a hard time breathing.

In French, people used to use the word *feu*, or *fire*, instead of *maison*, or *home*, to count, for instance, the number of houses in a town or a village. It is easy to see why: a house was first defined by its fireplace (a home is also a hearth), with so many chimneys signifying so many homes.

The word *feu* is also used to designate a person who has recently died. Yet these two instances of *feu* do not have the same origin; the first comes from the Latin *focus*, which designated a fireplace, while the second comes from *fatum* (fate, destiny) and indicates one whose destiny has been fulfilled. But I can't help but spot an invisible thread between these two fires, a sort of final blaze of one who leaves the Earth like dead wood rising up in sparks to the sky.

My father died while I was writing these pages. Put this way, you would think it a clear, discrete event, like saying: he hurt himself, he moved, he went on a trip – an act delimited in time, with a clear beginning and end. It was nothing of the sort: he took almost as long to die as I took to write this book; he just finished before me.

Sitting on either side of the dining room table, Austin and Lavinia are silent. She has placed between them a plate of oatcakes, a small bowl of raspberry meringues, and sugared shortbreads, as she would for a guest. In this house where he spent the early years of his life, he feels less than a visitor: a stranger. When did he stop feeling at home within these walls?, he wonders, as he takes a cookie to keep up a front. Was it when Emily died that the house stopped recognizing him?

As if reading his mind, Lavinia asks, 'Why was Susan so set on meeting here rather than at your house?'

He shrugs. Who knows why Susan does anything. He stopped trying to understand a long time ago. When she knocks at the door, they both get up to answer it, glad to have something to do.

Susan holds in her arms an enormous drawer filled with odds and ends. Austin wants to take it from her, but she refuses with a movement of her shoulders and goes to place her load on the table, next to the cookies.

'What have you brought us?' Lavinia asks, in a tone she hopes is cheerful. 'You're not moving, are you?'

Neither Austin nor Susan smile at this comment, and Lavinia bites her cheek, realizing this question might have already come up between them.

'Have a seat,' she says, but her guest remains standing.

'I have given some thought to this collection you are making with Emily's poems,' Susan begins, addressing her sister-in-law, while Austin pretends to be interested in a raisin in an oatcake.

Lavinia realizes that he has not thought to inform his wife of the identity of the second person to whom the project has been entrusted. All the things these people don't say to each other is exhausting.

'A cup of tea?' she suggests, and she fills the cup without waiting for a response.

'I've thought it over,' Susan continues, 'and I don't think it's a good idea.'

'Oh?'

'Well, not like that.'

'Sugar?'

'You both know as well as I do, Emily didn't just write poems, but also dozens, hundreds of letters, and those she never wanted to hide. Austin, you kept some too. I didn't throw out a single one; they span decades, ferociously funny, brilliant. Her herbarium would be at home in a natural history museum. She spent her youth picking four-leaf clovers, drying sprigs of jasmine and wild roses. Even later in life, she knew how to find treasures that no one else could see.'

Her hands trembling, she gradually takes from the drawer the things she is talking about: bundles of handwritten letters, cards on which are glued specimens of plants with their name written in Emily's pointed writing, dried flowers. Susan flips through the pages on which the flowers still seem mysteriously alive.

'This is also Emily's poetry; it was all this at the same time.'

She continues pulling from the drawer sand dollars, polished pebbles, a bird's nest, a grey stone streaked with white, like a magician would pull a string of scarves from a hat.

'All this should be included in the book, not just the poems that were her secrets. It would be like claiming to make a book about the moon and not showing its dark side.'

The papers and objects are towered on the table, threatening the meringues. Lavinia and Austin stare at each other, hoping the other will speak.

'But Susan, how in the devil do you want all this to fit in a book?' Austin finally asks in the calm, low voice he uses to address his subordinates and that happens to exasperate his wife.

'If it can fit in a drawer, it can fit in a book,' she replies.

Lavinia thinks to herself of all the things found in drawers that have no business in books: socks, underwear, insects, candle stubs. But the idea might not be that ridiculous – it's just that it is too late to entertain it. She nonetheless enjoys imagining for a moment Higginson's handsome desk covered with clusters of lilacs, birds' nests, and polished stones.

'Well,' Austin says, 'Lavinia will certainly give it some thought, isn't that right?'

'Certainly.'

'Emily is here,' Susan insists. 'Not just in her poems.'

She points to the empty drawer from which a moth emerges, awkwardly flapping its short pale wings, searching for light.

Without having taken a sip of tea, Susan returns the papers and the small objects to the drawer with dignity, turns on her heels to leave, but stops near the door to say over her shoulder, addressing her husband and sister-in-law without looking at either of them, 'Promise me that the name of that woman will not appear anywhere on Emily's book.'

'Sit down, please, so we can talk,' Lavinia implores.

'No.'

One would think she had decided that the chairs were her personal enemies.

'There is so much work to do already,' Lavinia eventually stammers, deeply uncomfortable. 'Best to see what Mr. Higginson thinks.'

They are equal in stature, but Susan seems to grow taller as she straightens to answer. 'Very well. I will wait until you settle the matter with him.'

Her tone is final. She has on her side all the pain in the world, and the dignity of a person who has refused to sit down.

Two days later, in Higginson's office, it is Lavinia's turn to plead the case.

'My dear Mr. Higginson, you must promise me that Mabel's name will not appear on the book.'

He seems surprised, but not unpleasantly so. He has felt the names were jostling for attention on this book.

'That is delicate, my dear madam, and no doubt the matter should have been settled earlier, but I will do everything in my power to see to it.'

The next day, he summons Mabel and addresses the question right away.

'My dear Mrs. Todd, it will not be possible to mention your collaboration on the cover. Your contribution is invaluable, make no mistake, but is not the only important name in this case that of the author?'

She is pale with rage, disappointment, and humiliation.

'But your name will appear, won't it?'

'Yes, well, that is not the same thing. My name signals to the learned that this is a serious publication that went through a rigorous editing process. It offers the book the seal of quality. What will readers learn from your name?'

'This book is mine as much as yours, as much as Emily's. I will not be pushed into the shadows.'

'It is not a question of pushing you into the shadows. It is just that the spotlight should not be on you.'

As he speaks these words, he gently guides her to the door.

That evening, Mabel tells Austin of the scandalous injustice just done to her. Austin, who detests conflict in all forms, tries to see if there is a way to straddle the fence.

'But is it that important, in the end, to see your name on the cover? You and I know very well what your contribution is. Is that not enough? Why the need to flaunt it?'

'Because not everyone can be Emily Dickinson.'

Austin wants to hold her close to reassure her, but rather than drowning her fear in his embrace, Mabel pulls away and, unsteady, tries to find the balance to hold herself perfectly straight, as if she were walking on a wire.

❧

The circle is closed, we are back in the parlour of Homestead with Austin and Lavinia, the players having consulted each other in serial sets of two, without ever meeting as a group. The last time they were all together in a room was at Emily's funeral. It takes death to bring them together.

'You can't take this away from her,' Austin argues to his sister. 'She has been working on it for months, as you know very well … Imagine poor David, who spent entire evenings with her deciphering the writing, while Higginson continued to work quietly on writing his articles ... '

'This is the first time I have ever heard you worry about poor David,' Lavinia points out to stall.

But Austin is right, and she knows it; it would be dishonest to erase Mabel's presence. However, Susan is also right not to want to see the name of her husband's mistress side by side for all eternity with that of her best friend, as if even death is taking a turn at betraying her.

The question keeps her up several nights in a row, until she finds the solution, one disarming in its simplicity.

The first print run of the book, dated November 12, 1890, will be limited to ten copies, which Lavinia will divide between Susan and herself. The remaining five hundred copies will bear Mabel's name, but Susan will never know, or will pretend she doesn't know. It won't be hard; she has grown accustomed to other people's lies.

Susan now forces herself to go out every day, although without pleasure. Most often, she contents herself with doing the rounds of the garden ten times, like prisoners who walk in circles in the yard, never going anywhere. Today, the clouds are heavy in the sky, and a fine mist floats over the streets and fields, but for the first time she pushes herself as far as the little woods that separates her property from that of the Todds. Among the trees, she spots, distant and elusive, a delicate pale shadow, which disappears behind a curtain of fog. Her heart leaps and starts to race. Which of her two ghosts have come to visit her? Silently, so as not to alarm them, she advances toward the apparition.

The little ghost briefly reappears before disappearing again among the birches. This time, Susan has time to make out the corolla of a skirt, and long dark hair. Emily. She brings her hand to her chest and closes her eyes. When she opens them, a flesh-and-blood little girl is standing in front of her, staring at her with her big dark eyes. She looks worried.

'Are you okay?' she asks.

She has twigs in her hair, and her smock and knees are wet, her ankle boots crusted in mud.

'I'm fine, thank you. What are you doing here?'

'I come here almost every day. It's the enchanted forest.'

'I see. And what is your name?'

'Millicent.'

This time, her ribs contract. Of course, it is that woman's young daughter. How had she not thought of it before? But the little girl keeps looking at her with curious, attentive eyes. She asks, in turn, 'And what is your name?'

'Susan.' She can't help adding, 'Would you like a hot chocolate by chance?'

They walk together toward Evergreens with the same quiet step. Millicent, who sees everything, points out to Susan a grove in the shape of a bear, a cloud in the same blue grey as the plumage of a jay, a perfectly round, shining pebble, which she slips in her pocket to add to her treasures.

In the empty house, Susan shows her into the parlour and rings for a hot chocolate. They hang the wet stockings and smock in front of the fireplace grate before sitting down on either side of the low table. Her feet tucked under her on the velvet armchair, Millicent remarks, 'I have never been inside your house, even though I see it every day.'

'That's true. And what do you think, now that you have seen it from the inside?'

Millicent takes in the plush carpets, the marble fireplace, the grand piano, the portraits in their frames with ornate gilding, the large crystal chandelier, and answers, plunging her eyes into Susan's, such that she doesn't know whether the little girl is talking about the house or Susan herself, 'It is a bit sad, I think.'

Susan does not disagree. She serves her little guest and continues to ask her questions.

'What do you want to do when you grow up?'

'I would like to visit every country in the world. And the stars, too. And you?'

Susan is speechless. If her life had depended on it, she wouldn't know how to answer the question. To avoid lying, she sidesteps it. 'I am already grown up, you know.'

'Does being grown up mean not wanting anything anymore?'

'Tell me, what are your favourite games?' Susan asks, avoiding the question again.

The little girl shrugs, before offering, 'I play the violin ...' Then a smile brightens her face. 'I love books.'

'Ah. Well, that's a happy coincidence.'

Susan gets up and takes from the low bookshelf a book with a fawn cover, which she shows the little girl. Millicent reads the title without faltering. 'The Adventures of Tom Sawyer.'

'Would you like to take it home?'

'May I?'

'You may, but on one condition; you must come back to return it when you are done and tell me what you thought of it.'

Her hot chocolate finished, her clothes dry, the little girl leaves, hugging the book to her heart. Susan follows her for a moment through the window. And then something in her gives way, collapses, and she cries all the tears she has left to cry.

Mabel walks in town, head high, her little heels clicking on the sidewalk, stooped to the side under the weight of her load. The machine is so heavy that she has to stop and put it down before continuing on her way. She feels people staring at her; everyone is aware of the scandalous truth. Mabel Loomis Todd, not content just to betray her husband – that charming young man so fascinated by the stars – is cuckolding him with Austin Dickinson, untouchable twice over, first because he is a Dickinson, then because he is the husband of Susan, ruling mother of the town, who has already suffered so much. She hears behind her back, 'It's that woman, you know …'

She has become *that woman*. Now that she has lost her name, all she has left is her book.

In the dining room, she takes out of her box the heavy Hammond machine she has borrowed. It is imposing. Thirty-three keys with combinations of numbers and letters are set in a half moon on a blond wood base. Each of the keys is connected to a small metal hammer at the end of which are sculpted the characters that will strike, through an inked ribbon, the sheet of paper that is rolled around an iron tube.

She runs her hands over the different parts of the machine, hitting one after the other the letters of the name she goes by in her dreams: Mabel Loomis Dickinson. Then she leans in closer to the mysterious machine to smell the mechanism, the fragrance of which reminds her vaguely of the scent of a storm, just before the lightning strike, a mixture of wood and metal.

She picks a poem at random from the dozens that have already been transcribed by hand, types it with care, and is astonished to see the printed characters, equal and perfect, recognizable to anyone, appear on the white sheet. They are already the words of a book. She stops for a moment, pulls the sheet from the roll that holds it in place, gently brushes her finger over the letters that have lightly bit into the paper. She closes her eyes, continues to follow the text with her finger. Emily's poems can be read even by someone who is blind.

Very early on, Higginson had decreed that the poems would have to be given titles.

'It is preferable to choose a word that does not appear in the poem,' he advised.

'Why?'

'To avoid repetition.'

Perplexed, Mabel had nodded her head. It seems to her that slapping a title on each poem would diminish the meaning and significance, and that, additionally, if Emily had wanted them to have titles, she would have taken the care to choose them herself, but she doesn't have the courage to oppose him, as he is so confident.

Higginson had also told her that the poems would have to be organized by theme. Bent over her transcriptions, she tries to separate the texts according to whether they talk about love, death, or birds. The three piles overlap. She could distribute them at random and the result would be essentially the same.

The night before, when they met, she had tried to argue that it would be better to arrange the poems in the order in which they were written, which can be deduced from the changes in the handwriting, so as to follow the path of Emily's existence – even if it means asking for help from correspondents to whom Emily wrote throughout her life (she did not mention the name *Susan*). A wasted effort.

'Try to group the ones that talk about flowers,' Higginson suggested, as if he were suggesting she make a rock garden to calm her nerves.

The poems that talk about flowers, obviously, are the same ones that talk about love, death, or birds. Emily never writes about any one thing or from any one place; she writes from alongside love, from behind death, from inside the bird.

Day after day, Mabel slowly forges a path through the forest of poems, seeking the best way to move from one to the other so they respond to and illuminate each other. It is not for nothing that the word *clear* can apply to both language and land. This book, she can tell, will be a labyrinth where all paths lead to the centre and not to the exit. Exit to do what, when there are continents to explore in the spaces between words.

That afternoon, she is making good progress in her work, but David is expecting a colleague and his wife for dinner, and she will soon have to put away her notes, banish the type-writer, move the papers she has spread out on the table so she can see them all at once. Three, four, five times a week when evening comes she feels as though she is unravelling the work woven during the day. The guests arrive, Mabel is charming, the guinea fowl delicious, but the whole time they are there, she continues to think about Emily's poems, which await her in their boxes, like pieces of a puzzle.

The next morning, rather than spreading out the contents of the boxes and cartons on the dining room table, she takes them up to the attic of the house where, in a small maid's bedroom unoccupied since they hired a girl from town who goes home every night to sleep, hat boxes and lamps with faded shades had been accumulating. Mabel asks the maid to clear out the room.

'Where should I put everything?'

'I don't care. In the cellar. Or keep it all. Here, do you like this hat?' she asks, holding out an emerald-green confection with a long peacock feather sticking out of it.

She then has her dressing table brought up, on which she sets the typewriter, and one of the low parlour tables, where she fans out the poems. And then she closes the door behind her. Here, Higginson can't come to tell her what to do.

She works until she is bleary-eyed and her fingertips are raw, in the yellow glow of the lamp and the white light of the poems. And why, in the end? Who will remember her when she is gone? Why worry about posterity, why does she care about the opinion people as yet unborn will have of her in a hundred years? But aside from the fleeting embraces she shares with Austin, books remain the only way she has found not to die completely.

Words are not alive and yet, for months, every time Mabel rereads one of Emily's short poems, she feels there is a second heart beating between her ribs. Maybe this is how you live a hundred lives without shattering everything; maybe it is by living in a hundred different texts. One life per poem.

⁂

The room is tiny, the smallest of the house, but it is the only one that is hers alone – and the only one, aside from the kitchen, where she never sets foot, that doesn't have a mirror. On the wall, there are neither prints nor photos. Mabel goes into this blank room in the morning, has a sandwich brought to her at lunch, and only goes back down at the end of the afternoon.

It feels like she will soon reach her goal. Sometimes it seems like the book is complete, but then doubt immediately assails her; something is still missing that she is unable to name, but she is sure she will know it when she sees it.

One morning, when David is off on a walk with Millicent, the doorbell rings. Mabel half stands to check who it is through the window and recognizes at a glance the tall silhouette of Austin, his hat in hand. To her own surprise, for a moment she hesitates rather than rushing to answer the door. Then she looks at herself as if from the outside, sits back down in her chair, and plunges back into Emily's poems. It is the first time in her life she has preferred the company of another woman, dead or alive, to that of her lover.

When Lavinia and Holden awaken at the same time, the sun has been up for hours. Alarmed, she throws back the sheet and sits up in her bed, bringing a hand to her hair, as if she could, with a gesture, redo her chignon. He pulls her gently until she is lying with her head on the pillow.

'Don't get up. I'll go make coffee.'

He gets up, puts on his pants, and goes downstairs while she stretches out between the rumpled sheets. She hears the grinder and the water running, and then the delicious smell of coffee and toast rises to her nose, and she sighs in comfort. She has never stayed in bed so late; it is the first time in her adult life that someone is making her breakfast. Is this what it would be like to have a husband?

During the day, he tends to the garden, trims the hedges, hoes the flower beds that were abandoned for the vegetable garden. He scatters little pebbles along the pathways, weeds, prunes the old sycamores of the dead branches that are at risk of giving out in the next strong wind. From the road, he looks like an ordinary hired hand. Lavinia is careful not to speak to him when busybodies are likely to come upon them.

They meet again in the evening. She sets in front of him what she has spent the day cooking: poussin with prunes, the flesh so tender it comes apart on the fork, salmon mousse, goose liver pâté infused with cognac, strawberry shortcake, which was Emily's favourite dessert. He devours everything with gusto.

She wakes up in the middle of the night, her heart pounding. And yet silence reigns in the large house; through the window, the night is calm, the moon is high in the sky. She closes her eyes again. Her blood is beating in her temples. Holden turns over in his sleep, places a forearm heavy as lead on Lavinia's chest, and she tries to free herself by wriggling away. She ends up lifting his hand and putting the arm on the chest of the sleeper. She closes her eyes, tries to think of peaceful things – balls of wool, ham quiche, cattails on the edge of a pond, a steaming cup of tea – but it is futile. The mattress sags under Holden's weight, and she can't help but be sucked into the depression. To remain level is an effort that is wholly incompatible with sleep. She moves as far away as she can, even lying on the very edge of the bed. When she opens her eyes, she sees the floorboards. She had never noticed that they are irregularly spaced. Holden snorts like horses sometimes do in the stables, a half sneeze, and starts to gently snore. The snoring takes up all the space in Lavinia's ears; thunder could clap in the bedroom and she wouldn't hear it; it fills her head like a liquid fills a jar, assails her from within.

In horror this time, she thinks: is this what it would be like to have a husband?

⁊

In mid-summer, the Mercers set up a maze in their cornfield and invite the townspeople to lose themselves in it. The children rush in, trembling with delight, and even the adults enjoy losing their way in the narrow corridors that smell pleasantly of hay and sun stored up over the summer. The route is not very elaborate, but it is still convoluted enough to take more than a half hour and many about-faces to reach the end.

'We should go,' Holden suggests to Lavinia, as they are weeding side by side.

She starts. 'You have lost your mind.'

She doesn't need to add: *What would people say?*

He shrugs. 'We could go at night.'

They go that very night, like thieves, winding down the deserted streets with a single lamp between them. Lavinia feels like she is twelve years old again. The maze is not guarded, of course, or closed in any way. They enter, taking care that the flame from their lamp does not set fire to the dry ears of corn. If orientation is difficult during the day, in the dark it becomes almost impossible; they can see only three feet ahead of them and do not see the dead ends until they bump into them with their noses. Holden's dog, who has accompanied them, is of no use; he disappears for long minutes before reappearing, delighted, running circles around them.

'We'll never do it. We'll have to wait for sunrise,' Lavinia eventually sighs, but Holden won't be dissuaded.

He is off again, muttering the directions to himself, noting the non-existent landmarks, and she has no choice but to follow. After many minutes, they finally emerge in a cleared square where a scarecrow is standing.

'You see?' Holden says, excited. 'You can't get discouraged!'

Lavinia acquiesces in silence. She straightens the hat on the head of the straw figure, who thanks her with a wink – the other eye has fallen to the ground. They are still surrounded by tall ears whose dry leaves crackle with the slightest gust of wind. They haven't found the exit by any means. They have reached the centre.

At the age of fifty-four, in the middle of the maze, surrounded by the darkness, Lavinia is struck by a keen awareness of having reached the middle of her life – the moment when, believing we have reached our goal, we realize we are lost. The following question then arises: does the second half of existence have to be devoted to trying to find one's way again, or to getting more thoroughly lost? Do we have to retrace our steps to find the way out of the maze? And what if she simply decided to lie down there, at the scarecrow's feet, and also dream of the blazes of the coming winter?

She doesn't know how to inhabit this third season she has been given. She lifts her eyes to the sky, which, in this moment, seems to be the only way out. The stars that shine in it are infinitely distant, insignificant grains of sugar.

One evening, as they are drinking tea after having eaten at the kitchen table (they never sit in the dining room, which is where the ghosts eat), Holden gets up and goes to get an old deck of cards from his satchel.

'I'm going to read your future,' he announces to Lavinia, who does not let herself be impressed.

'At my age, there is more past than future. It will be easy to read.'

He ignores her, shuffles the cards, holds out the deck for her to cut, then shuffles again.

'Did you know,' Lavinia asks, 'that at the beginning of the French colony, when they were short on coins, they used playing cards?'

'How did that work?'

'There was no printer yet on the continent, and barely any paper either. But every home had a deck of cards. They were requisitioned, and some cards were cut up; a whole card was worth four pounds, a half was worth two, and a quarter was worth fifteen cents, an official signed it and that was that.'

'Turn one over,' Holden says, holding out the pack.

It is the eight of clubs.

'What does it mean?' Lavinia asks.

'I don't know yet. You have to pick six others and think of a question.'

Despite herself, Lavinia is tempted to ask what will become of Emily's book, which is perhaps, when you get down to it, the only future that remains to her.

She picks the cards one by one at random, solemnly places them on the table: jack of spades, king of hearts, nine of diamonds, seven of hearts, when a gust of air from the window lifts the cards and scatters them haphazardly on the floor, the ones she picked and the rest of the pack. Holden bends to pick them up, but Lavinia holds him back.

'Leave it. It's perfect like that,' she says.

They have a fortune spread out at their feet.

Feathered things

Birds
Inkwells
Boas
Pillows
Hope

There is another way to escape the maze: by air. When Daedalus and Icarus are preparing to leave the labyrinth, with their wings made of feathers and wax on their backs, the father warns his son: 'Be careful not to fly too close to the sun: its heat will melt the wax and burn your wings. But be careful as well not to get too close to the sea, because its humidity will weigh down your feathers and make you founder.'

The airspace is infinitely narrow, delimited by two immensities – like life, between two abysses. Daedalus launches himself outside the labyrinth, he glides through the blue, and Icarus jumps in turn. He has never felt so free in his life. Soon, taking his eyes off his father, who is showing him the way, he ascends toward the blue of the sky, farther and farther from what he knows, less and less himself. In the headiness of feeling suddenly weightless, he approaches the rays of the sun. The wax that holds the feathers together starts to melt without him noticing. He flies higher still, until his wings come undone and fall to pieces. He falls with them to the sea, is drowned in the ocean. Although seemingly mutually exclusive, both the father's threats came true: he succumbed both to the sun and the sea. He fell twice.

Of course, one can blame Icarus; he should have listened to his father, been careful, resisted the headiness of flight.

But we might also wonder why Daedalus and his son did not launch themselves from the top of the tower in the middle of the night. The moon would have provided light without danger.

࠾

Some things are visible only at night: stars, bats, fireflies. Others exist only in the day. These include shadow, that little night.

࠾

The word *fall* refers at once to the act of falling, the thing itself (a waterfall), and the result of the action. A single word for verb, subject, and object; fall is a sentence in itself. It is the whole story.

The etymology of the French verb *tomber*, or *to fall*, is uncertain. One hypothesis is that it is an onomatopoeia mimicking the sound of an object hitting the ground (*tumb*). Another, more appealing, connects the word to the Old English *tumben*, which means 'to pirouette,' 'to twirl.'

࠾

They dropped like Stars —
They dropped like flakes —
Like Petals from a Rose —

Only Emily Dickinson could compare soldiers falling on the battlefield to flower petals or snowflakes, show them whirling, fluttering, infinitely light, scintillating, and fragile. Only Dickinson could have us see death as a dance.

~ 166 ~

We have all had dreams where we suddenly lose our footing and fall, like vertigo that grows deeper with time and distance travelled, an endless fall, because in dreams, you never reach the ground.

'You can't die in your dreams. If you die in your dream, you die in real life.'

This is what people used to say when I was a child, convinced it was true. I took great care over the years never to die in a dream. I am not sure I succeeded.

She is there, immobile in the corner of the dining room, a lightly mocking smile on her lips. Over her shoulder flutters a hummingbird with shimmering emerald and carmine plumage. Millicent jumps when she sees her, but the apparition places a finger to her mouth to ask for silence, and the little girl says nothing. Mabel has come down with one of the last problematic poems and is debating with David about the best word to choose from among the handful of synonyms to insert in the middle of a verse crossed out three times.

The word that is troubling her is the third in the second verse, and there are a host of possibilities.

'First she writes *delusive*,' David points out.

'Yes, but she crossed it out. What is written darker, with a firmer stroke, is *dissembling*.'

The apparition gently shakes her head.

'Maybe, but proceeding logically, it is the term the furthest out that would be the last one written. So it should read: *dissolving*.'

The apparition seems to silently sigh. She turns her head to the side and, making the same gesture, Millicent discovers that another word is written on the edge of the paper, vertically, with such a light pencil that it is almost translucent. Nothing suggests that it belongs to this verse, but the little girl whispers, as if to herself, this word: *revolving*.

The apparition nods. The bird lands on her shoulder, stops frantically beating its wings for a moment. Millicent dares to ask, out loud this time, 'What if *revolving* were the right word?'

The adults don't hear her. She repeats herself, and her father thanks her. 'We're not having difficulty making it out, my love. This time we are trying to choose, it's different.'

Emily and Millicent, both reduced to silence, exchange looks and agree: people don't listen enough to the dead or to children – or to birds.

Higginson, when Mabel writes to ask for his advice, is categorical: *When there are several possibilities for one word, choose the one that will offer the clearest expression.*

Yet, in studying the texts, Mabel understands that Emily seems to have done exactly the opposite: starting from the expected term, she crosses it out to gradually move away, one word at a time, until she picks one that has only a distant relationship of connotation with the first, like the echo of an idea she wants to plant not on the page but in the reader's mind. If she has to choose between naming a thing and evoking its shadow, the shadow will always win.

What Mabel senses and Higginson still refuses to see is that Emily only ever wrote half a poem; the other half belongs to the reader, it is the voice that rises up in each person as a response. And it takes these two voices, the living and the dead, to make the poem whole.

In the field between the two houses, Millicent picks daisies, clover, and handfuls of dandelions, which are her favourite flowers, even though people call them weeds. When her bunch gets so big she has a hard time holding it in one hand, she rings at the door of Evergreens and holds out the scruffy bouquet to Susan, with *The Adventures of Tom Sawyer*, which she devoured not once, but twice, as she announces. Susan puts the humble flowers in a vase with care, as if she were arranging the most precious roses. She leads the little girl to the parlour where *The Adventures of Huckleberry Finn* awaits her on the low table, and proposes: 'Would you like me to read to you what comes next?'

Millicent is big; it has been a long time – years – since anyone read to her, but she accepts all the same, climbs into an armchair and, curled up against the cushion, listens to Susan, who begins.

You don't know about me, without you have read a book by the name of The Adventures of Tom Sawyer, *but that ain't no matter. That book was made by Mr. Mark Twain, and he told the truth, mainly.*

Millicent is hooked. That books can tell the truth, *mainly*, had never crossed her mind. Are they like adults, always lying a little? But if they admit they are not quite telling the truth, is it still a lie? The hours go by and neither notices the light growing dimmer in the room. They don't think to light a lamp. The afternoon comes to an end, and Susan has read more than a third of the novel when she stops, half expecting to find Millicent asleep. But the little girl is staring at her, wide-eyed.

'Then what?' she asks.

'Then what is that you have to go home. But take the book, if you like. You can keep reading it at home. And you'd better go or your parents will worry.'

Millicent grabs the book and hurries to the door. There, rather than leaving, she turns to Susan and, giving the book back to her, asks, 'Could I leave it with you instead and come back so you can read it to me?'

When Millicent pushes open the door to The Dell, no one has been worried about her absence. David is at the college, and Mabel is lost in her work. She goes up to her bedroom, takes out her notebook of lists, and on the *My best friends* page, beside Emily's name, writes another one with a determined hand: *Mrs. Susan.*

Two days later, it is Lavinia who rings the bell at Evergreens to show Susan the blank book Higginson has entrusted to her. It is a volume similar to the one where Emily's poems will be printed, but its pages are blank, a mock-up to offer a preview of the size, weight, cover, grain, and thickness of the paper.

No one answers, so Lavinia leaves the book at the door, along with a short, hastily scribbled note: *For Emily's book.*

Susan discovers it only at the end of the day. She weighs the book in her hands, breathes it in before opening it and flipping through its hundred blank pages. This book of snow is exactly what she had dreamed of.

Back home, Lavinia takes out the flour, lard, butter, and sugar, which she places on the kitchen table. She puts on her apron, takes the stoneware bowl, a knife, her wooden spoon, and it is only at that moment, as she is getting ready to cut the butter in cubes, that she realizes that deep down she has never liked pies. Her father gobbled them up; her mother liked nothing better than a cherry pie; Austin always had a predilection for the mincemeat pies she made at Christmas; Emily liked apricot tarts. Holden devours them all, sweet or savoury, no matter the filling, the spices, the seasoning. And so, for years, she thought she also liked pies, when she took no pleasure in eating them.

She gets two eggs from the icebox, with the heavy cream. For months she had kept a block of chocolate in the pantry, not knowing what she would do with it; now she unwraps it carefully, bending to breathe in the aroma. On a wooden board, she grates it into fine shavings, tips them into a saucepan that she sets in a *bain-marie*. She slowly lets the chocolate melt, then, for good measure, she adds a spoonful of brandy.

She separates the two eggs, setting aside the yolks, which she will use later for mayonnaise; she beats the whites until they are silken and satiny, adds the sugar, and continues beating. In another bowl, she whips the cream into gently curved peaks. She combines the two mixtures, pours in the melted chocolate, then takes out six dessert cups to pour in the concoction, but changes her mind.

Undoing the ties of her apron, she sits at the kitchen table in front of a large bowlful of chocolate mousse and digs in with the large, finely wrought silver spoon she normally uses for serving on important occasions.

Night falls over Homestead. The robin comes one last time to look at itself in the window before going back to its nest. Darkness falls like a curtain in the kitchen where Lavinia, under the golden circumference of the lamp, abandons the spoon to plunge her fingers into the chocolate mousse, with an appetite she hasn't had since childhood.

When, many years later, the doctor who pronounced Emily dead comes to lean over her sister's face, eyes closed but lips still slightly parted, he will note in his still precise writing, under the heading 'Cause of death,' *enlarged heart*. A heart too big.

Pieces of wood from a shipwreck tired of bobbing in the sea wash up on a beach of round pebbles smooth as eggs. The ocean is calm, the waves lick the sand as they whisper. Gilbert is in the water up to his waist. Closer to shore, Sophia and Emily lift the hems of their skirts to walk; their ankles are milky white. Carlo joins them at full gallop, sending up sprays of water, and swims to the child who continues to move further from shore. They aren't worried as they watch him head into the distance; what could happen to him now?

Sophia stops for a moment, bends over, plunges her arm into the clear water and pulls out a blue-white shell as big as her fist and presses it to her ear. She listens for a long time and then passes it to Emily, who listens in turn. Gilbert comes back, with Carlo ahead of him, and he also presses the large conch to his little ear. Inside, the distant ringing of the bells of Amherst can be heard.

She gets out of bed while the house is plunged in silence. She is still in her clothes. She has no difficulty walking along the corridor, going down the fourteen steps of the large staircase, then noiselessly pushing open the door. Once outside, the moon lights her way.

She easily clambers onto the white fence, the rails of which seem perfectly placed to help her climb. When she reaches the top, for a moment she sits astride, a foot on either side. It is not too late to go back. An owl hoots, the frogs make sounds like tiny chimes. A cloud passes in front of the moon, and for a second she no longer sees her shadow. She uses that moment to stand on the fence, and from there, to hoist herself onto the lowest branch of the tall maple. The others are within reach; it's almost too easy to climb up to the window that is ajar. As she goes, she disturbs a few bats that flee, fluttering awkwardly, as if they were missing a wing or an eye. How could God, who had created the birds, give life to these poor creatures? Do they fly only at night because they know they are ugly?

The branch gives directly onto the window. The leaves must brush the pane at the slightest gust; no doubt their rustling accompanied the dreams of the woman who slept there. Millicent slides one leg into the opening; she lifts the window with her back and slips the rest of her body into the dark bedroom. She has never felt so flexible, so strong, so alive, as she does standing alone in this deserted room.

Millicent sits on the bed, runs her hand over the duvet. Looking through the window at the pale face of the moon, she whispers:

I'm Nobody. Who are you?
Are you – Nobody – too?
Then there's a pair of us!
Don't tell! they'd advertise, you know.

Millicent sits where Emily sat, takes a sheet of paper from the drawer. The ink has dried up in the inkwell, but Lavinia has left a glass of water in the room. Millicent pours in a few drops, and the paste grows lighter, the consistency of gouache.

She takes the pen, dips it in the ink, then places the tip on the paper. She closes her eyes. Whether it is her hand that is writing, her heart, or her head, the whole bedroom or the autumn night with its stars, its cicadas, and the wind that makes the maple leaves shiver, she couldn't say, but the poem is written, as if it had been left behind, forgotten in the room, just waiting for her to appear.

She blows on the paper to dry the ink, carefully folds and refolds it, until it is no bigger than the palm of her hand. She looks around the room to soak in every detail: the white bed, the candle, the mirror where she sees her face without recognizing it. She places her fingers gently on these eyes, this nose, this mouth that belong to her without being her. For a moment, she wants to lie down between the sheets, but some silent voice tells her that if she does, she might never get up again. So she leaves through the open window and goes back home with the moon as her only witness. In the sleeping house, she places the poem among the others that are piling up on Mabel's work table and that form, in the dark, a little mountain of light. She should be ashamed, perhaps, but she is too tired – too delighted.

In the morning, her mother is astonished to discover in the middle of a white sheet a quatrain that she has never seen, but she will nonetheless decipher it and transcribe it diligently, then insert it among Emily's poems in the manuscript she will soon present to Higginson. The other poems recognize it and move over to make room.

Somewhere, Millicent could swear, Emily is silently laughing.

That day, finally, the book is done.

The poems have been transcribed, corrected, ordered; the bundle of papers that Mabel reviews to get rid of the final typos will soon be reproduced in hundreds of copies, distributed in libraries, reviewed by journalists and academics. She will finally exist.

Mabel has dreamed a hundred times, a thousand times, of this moment when she will hold the printed pages in her hand. She imagined herself feeling a blend of pride, exaltation, joy, incredulity, wonder. But when the day finally comes that she can flip through the set of proofs to the title page on which her name stands outs, irrefutable, printed beside that of Emily Dickinson, she feels nothing but profound relief, as if she has just escaped some terrible jeopardy: obscurity. Not because the light is finally shining on her, as she so wanted, but because she has managed to relight a handful of stars that without her would have remained invisible.

When the collection finally appears on November 12, 1890, with Roberts Brothers, it is not made of jasmine, snow, or butterflies, as Susan dreamed. At first glance, it is a book that resembles any other, with paper pages, a cover of stretched pale fabric where a handful of blue flowers bow their heads under an invisible shower. The colour of the back cover, which is darker, bleeds onto the front, in a cut that suggests the waves of the ocean. It contains a lie, on the flyleaf: *edited by two of her friends.* But the rest is the truth.

In holding it in their hands for the first time, Lavinia, Susan, Mabel, and even Millicent half expect to feel the heart of the dead woman beating, as one would feel a feathered thing beating between one's fingers. In vain: her printed poems do not bring Emily back to life. But this book born after her opens up an eternity as large as a palm, one hundred and fifty-eight pages, a lantern to light the darkness.

Once the last page of the collection is turned, Millicent sits at her table, by candlelight. Through the window, the dead and living stars burn equally bright. She takes a blank new notebook from her drawer. She writes in it, with her left hand, the word *Poems*, then spends a long time looking at all that the first of these new, blank pages do not yet contain, this bit of infinity opened up for her by Miss Emily.

Susan holds the book to her heart for a long time before daring to lift the cover. *Open me carefully.*

The charm is intact, miraculous. In this fragile paper house, fires are burning. Emily did not live in an enchanted world; she was the enchantment.

Lavinia grips the book in her hands. It trembles.

She gently pushes open the door of Emily's room, where nothing has changed, where nothing will ever change. It is the end of the afternoon; the light that comes in through the window is filtered by the red leaves of the maple, the will-o'-wisps dancing on the desk and the floor. Lavinia sits on the bed, places the book on the pillow, which sags a little, as if under the weight of a bird. The curtain shivers for a moment from an invisible gust. Then Lavinia stands and goes back out, leaving the door ajar.

She died – this was the way she died;
And when her breath was done,
Took up her simple wardrobe
And started for the sun.

AUTHOR'S NOTE

This book came to me by the sea, in the sun, at the end of summer 2020. My daughter was playing in the shallow pools of water, and I was watching her from a distance, sitting on a flat rock. The sun was beating down, it was August, almost noon. My work was going nowhere. I was forcing myself to write every day, torn between four or five novels at different stages of incompletion, half of them started years earlier, others just begun. I was banging my head against all of them equally. I tied myself to them as if they were a chore, and every time I came away from them disappointed. This wasn't it. I didn't want to live in any of these worlds. I didn't believe in any of them.

We were at the end of the beach, which in a way is the end of the world. Looking up at the small houses outlined in the distance like a string cut out of paper, I understood in a flash that the world I was continuing to inhabit in my imagination, that I returned to as soon as I stopped forcing myself to take an interest in something else, the world to which I returned as instinctively as one would take the road home, was Emily Dickinson's Amherst. It was the first time I dared admit it to myself, and this observation was accompanied by an obvious conclusion: the story I had to write was the sequel to that one. But the absurd character of the enterprise was not lost on me – how could I expect to create a sequel to a book when the main character is dead? How could I expect to outlive Emily Dickinson?

A little ways away, Zoé was building a bridge, digging a tunnel, erecting a tower, detailing out loud each step of her creation, chatter I distractedly followed. The ocean had gone out so far that we almost couldn't see it, a dark blue line at the horizon. For a long moment, we were alone with the gulls, the plovers, and the clouds.

I started writing that day, waving off the question that was plaguing me, the answer to which ended up appearing to me, although months later, when I stopped searching: constructing what comes after death is what we do every day of our existence. It is called continuing to live.

While based on real people, the characters in this novel are essentially beings of fiction, whose actions, words, and feelings I wanted to imagine. I hope I will be forgiven for the liberties I have taken with the 'official' history of the publication of Emily Dickinson's poems; I respected the most important milestones.

Thank you to François Ricard, my first reader, always so exacting and generous. Thank you to Nadine Bismuth and Catherine Leroux for their invaluable comments. Thank you to Antoine Tanguay and Chloé Deschamps, who keep believing. Thank you to Fred and Zoé for sharing their lives with me.

Dominique Fortier is a novelist and translator. She has translated major Canadian voices, including Anne Michaels, Margaret Laurence, Mordecai Richler, and Heather O'Neill, and is a four-time finalist for the Governor General's Literary Award for translation. Her translation of O'Neill's *The Lonely Hearts Hotel* won the Cole Foundation Prize from the Quebec Writers' Federation. Her first novel, *Du bon usage des étoiles* (*On the Proper Use of Stars*), was nominated for a Governor General's Award and the Prix des Libraires du Québec, and *Au péril de la mer* (*The Island of Books*) won the Governor General's Award for French fiction. *Les villes de papier* (*Paper Houses*) won France's Prix Renaudot – Essai. Fortier is a member of the Fondation Prince Pierre de Monaco literary council. She divides her time between Montreal and Maine.

Rhonda Mullins is a Montreal-based translator who has translated many books from French into English, including Jocelyne Saucier's *And Miles To Go Before I Sleep*, Grégoire Courtois's *The Laws of the Skies*, Dominique Fortier's *Paper Houses*, and Anaïs Barbeau-Lavalette's *Suzanne*. She is a seven-time finalist for the Governor General's Literary Award for Translation, winning the award in 2015 for her translation of Jocelyne Saucier's *Twenty-One Cardinals*. Novels she has translated were contenders for CBC Canada Reads in 2015 and 2019, and *Suzanne* was a finalist for the 2018 Best Translated Book Award. Mullins was the inaugural literary translator in residence at Concordia University in 2018. She is a mentor to emerging translators in the Banff International Literary Translation Program.

Typeset in Jenson and Medino.

Printed at the Coach House on bpNichol Lane in Toronto, Ontario, on Zephyr Antique Laid paper, which was manufactured, acid-free, in Saint-Jérôme, Quebec, from second-growth forests. This book was printed with vegetable-based ink on a 1973 Heidelberg KORD offset litho press. Its pages were folded on a Baumfolder, gathered by hand, bound on a Sulby Auto-Minabinda, and trimmed on a Polar single-knife cutter.

Coach House is on the traditional territory of many nations, including the Mississaugas of the Credit, the Anishnabeg, the Chippewa, the Haudeno-saunee, and the Wendat peoples, and is now home to many diverse First Nations, Inuit, and Métis peoples. We acknowledge that Toronto is covered by Treaty 13 with the Mississaugas of the Credit. We are grateful to live and work on this land.

The image on page 168 is a fictionalized composite that uses Emily Dickinson's handwriting. It does not constitute a real document.

Translated by Rhonda Mullins
Edited by Alana Wilcox
Cover design by Ingrid Paulson
Interior design by Crystal Sikma
Author photo by Frederick Duchesne
Translator photo by Owen Egan

Coach House Books
80 bpNichol Lane
Toronto ON M5S 3J4
Canada

mail@chbooks.com
www.chbooks.com